Easy Living

Easy Living
stories

JESUS HARDWELL

EXILE
editions

Library and Archives Canada Cataloguing in Publication

Hardwell, Jesus, 1962-
    Easy living : stories / Jesus Hardwell.

ISBN 978-1-55096-224-6

    I. Title.

PS8615.A723E28 2011   C813'.6   C2011-901510-2

Design and Composition by Digital ReproSet mc
Cover Photo "State Street, Santa Barbara, California, 1981" © Chuck Koton
Typeset in Book Antiqua and Lucida at the Moons of Jupiter Studios
Printed in Canada by Imprimerie Gauvin

The publisher would like to acknowledge the financial assistance of
the Canada Council for the Arts and the Ontario Arts Council, which is
an agency of the Government of Ontario.

Conseil des Arts Canada Council
du Canada for the Arts

ONTARIO ARTS COUNCIL
CONSEIL DES ARTS DE L'ONTARIO

Printed and Bound in Canada in 2011
Published by Exile Editions Ltd.
144483 Southgate Road 14 – GD
Holstein, Ontario, N0G 2A0

Canadian Sales Distribution: U.S. Sales Distribution:
McArthur & Company   Independent Publishers Group
c/o Harper Collins   814 North Franklin Street
1995 Markham Road   Chicago, IL 60610
Toronto, ON M1B 5M8   www.ipgbook.com
toll free: 1 800 387 0117   toll free: 1 800 888 4741

for K, who knows.

Easy Living

So long as you didn't try to burn it down, or annoy your fellows with a knife or something, they left you alone at the Beacon. It was cheap, the bar made deliveries, and the shower worked. Ceiling fans like huge propellers sliced the light, and the Cuban guy at the desk when night came would close his mind like a bag over his face – you could watch it happen – and turn to stone. He was known as Jonah because he worked on a freighter, before he jumped. He was ill in some way and given to rages, but was mostly all right, and he'd let you in for free on occasion if you'd share, so generally I did when I had enough. It was home of sorts at the Beacon, and a fine place to get lost.

We had been there three or four days, me and the wife of an acquaintance, shoving everything we had inside us, including, when we could manage it, each other. Those were good days, full of high vacant fervour and disregard. There was a sweet raw taste to time, and the room itself, according to our mood, became a vast cathedral, or a small velvet box. It was pleasant whichever way, though most of who we were there and what we did I forget. But I remember the sheets had stars, hundreds of blue stars shattered all over. And I remember her breasts, how they buoyed, and the wet spikes of her nipples floured with coke. I jammed them up my nose and we floated off immense above ourselves, empty and marvellous.

That couldn't last, of course. We wore out, we aged, the drugs evaporated. Our throats dried. Our skins grew tight and tender, and what air remained was from the desert, and had quills. We were dogs really, dragging around what was left of us like we'd been run over and didn't have the sense to stop yet. The room was just a room, and she had a husband she was late to get back to.

Then one of us, by miracle, found some hash we'd trampled. It was heavy hash, import deluxe from Morocco. We didn't have a pipe, so we knived it. The burn through our heads was hot and cool together, with a delicate edge of ambush. Straight away we brightened, and pretty soon we were feeling almost repaired. She began to look all right again, quite clean and filthy at once, which I like.

So I grew my arm across the room to where she was, stark there on the bed with a leg up, watching my hand enlarge and sniff about to find her. I took her hair, the spattery twists of her hair flashing in rivulets, and twined it in my fist and wound, reeling her in until our foreheads banged. Then I said into her eyes that the room was on fire and we had twenty minutes to live. It wasn't much to give, but it struck her well somewhere and she clasped me down.

As we rocked I saw her face loosen and change. I watched it slide, dissolve, and then reform into three. It was her in the middle, and the two others beside rippling across, back and forth. They were emerging and blending so fast I couldn't make out if I knew them. It didn't matter. Their mouths were wide and lovely, they looked ready to sing, and everyone was smiling. We rowed and lolled. I swam on their tongues. And when I beckoned them they came and came and met me where I was, holding them there and waiting. When it was time the stars squeezed and blew apart. The force of it spasmed from my spine and bent me. It moaned me open and I gasped my love, my full helpless love for all of us happy there together. Then the bed swallowed and we drowned.

We slept some, we must have. When I woke it was me alone that surfaced. She was one again below me, a fragile wreck smashed out still and far beyond. I checked to see if she was breathing. She was, so it seemed all right to leave her. I got my clothes and shook them on. In her purse I found a compact and broke the mirror off. I laid it between her legs and combed my hair. When I left she was just starting to stir. In my mind I blew her a kiss, and added one for Jonah. Then I was gone and out into the fresh shock of the air, and walking along on the lighted carcass of the city at night.

I was headed for a bar I knew in a hotel by the harbour. There was fog in the streets, and spangles of snow had shaken loose and were swirling around. I hurried because I knew we could sit, Chummy and I, sit there and drink, and be warm and easy, and listen to the horns muscle in.

He was there, of course, at a table where the bar ended. He was always there when I knew him, except when he was working, which he wasn't much then. He wasn't too drunk and waved me over. Before I asked he said, "Pretty fine. Pretty fine and the same, my man. Yourself?" I said I was fine too, the finest, and I sat, and we ordered Coronas and lime.

The arm he'd waved with stayed suspended. It was a while before it fell and I looked for the tattoo on the back of his wrist that made him angry, and he might get rid of. It was true the trumpet was more a trombone and I thought the cigar in the end too much myself, but the mantis was well done. It looked stubborn and wise, and when he flexed it had a jaunt to it. He had never shot through the mantis and I was glad it wasn't gone.

The beer came and went and came again. Then Chummy asked what was I going to do, if I was going to do anything, about the wife. I said that was probably over.

"That's the way," he said. He'd had wives himself, and been married twice. "It's always done and finished, and then it isn't."

"Sure. But it's finished sometimes. You can see the skid marks." I liked talking left-handed like that, and trying to guess where he was going.

"Yeah, it stops. But you can't know when it does. So what you feel when you think it does is just yourself stringing yourself along and hoping. That's the way it is, my man, all the freaking way until you're dead. That's just the true smiling bitch of it."

This was a little beyond where I wanted to be at that time, so I had to agree, and we let it drop. Before it dropped, though, he said, "Sometimes I think you trust too much."

"So you do? And what does that mean?"

"I really do, and that's what it means."

"Well all right," I said. "I'll put a watch on that, and you can show me the coin for the next round."

"Fair enough. I'm with you there, my man." Then he added, "You realize I'm just slinging it, right?"

"Sure. Everything's good." And it was, even though I knew he meant it then. I held up two fingers, a touch apart. "We're like this."

"I see," he said. "Let it be tight like that then."

Chummy left for a bit to make a call for an arrangement. My mind wandered and I let it stretch. I thought of the wife – her name was Rebecca; Savannah, professionally – and how much she might tell her husband. He was a bit of a dealer and a bit of a thief – nothing serious, just what was easy – and a decent guy despite. Then I wondered why it was, although you couldn't be sure what even the decent were capable of, why it was really that I didn't care at all what she told. I didn't get far with that, so I forgot it and looked around the bar.

It wasn't crowded. The locals were drunks mostly – hawk-faced and devastated, hoarding their tables as though they were precious aeries of refuge – and the others were drop-ins, tourists from the cruise ships. I thought I heard some German, but it was probably just Texans. They were blond and loud and what I could see of their faces bored me, so I waited for Chummy and twirled a bottle on the table. When it stopped it pointed at his chair, at the coat he'd draped over. It was a huge coat, raccoon, and still in fair condition. For a time he kept a gun in the pocket over his heart. It wasn't for use, not directly. But it could solve a situation sometimes. Relax it, I mean, before it happened. But then, the guy who told me that hanged himself in a cell, so there you go. The gun had been pawned for a while, but he kept the coat all the time I knew him. One summer, the whole summer, he wore it through the heat. He said he enjoyed it – the animal feel and breathing of the heat – of course, he was also timing everyone's conversation with a stopwatch then. I never saw him worse, and he couldn't play, but when he could he was something rare.

When he was more or less fit for a time and playing regularly in a not-at-all-bad quartet, I went to hear him in a club downtown. It was well after the hour and the rest of them were on the stand already. They tuned and waited, traded a few runs and waited some more, pretending without trying to be convincing that it was part of the show. But Chummy wouldn't come. He just stood at the back, in the raccoon coat against the wall as though nailed there, cradling his trumpet like a damaged child. He stared straight ahead, but what he saw wasn't anything there in the solid sense. In fact, you'd have sworn he was completely blind. There was a clear chance of an incident, I suppose, but it didn't happen, and after a while a Korean girl I wasn't familiar with came and got him. She led him shuffling, testing each step like he was feeling for where the cliff was, up through the tables, through the smoke and the elbows and the noise. It was a long way, and he was slow, but he made it to the chair they had for him and gentled himself in. I didn't think he'd be able to haul back from wherever he was, but when they started he was right there, resurrected and sure.

The first notes were serene, with a lot of space between them. Then he played some half ones fast and stricken. He went on alternating like that, stacking them apart as though he were building two separate things. Toward the end he mixed them and soldered, and they held and made a kind of arch. For a moment we all passed naked through into some place we didn't belong, but was ours anyway until it ended.

That's what I liked about the music, and about Chummy too. Everything was as possible as nothing, and you weren't obliged to choose or be responsible. It was enough to survive and try to know a little of who you were, if you cared. We always agreed on that. But it wasn't the type of thing you would say straight out, or even want to really.

So when Chummy came back at last and gave me the good word on the arrangement, we tossed around whether the foghorns should be thought horns, or a whole section of basses that the wind bowed. We decided on both and drank some more and considered the waitress. She was young and we admired her nylons, the soft brush when she walked, and her wrists' efficiency. She had china bones. Then we switched to scotch and talked of Clifford Brown and how rotten it was what happened. Chummy had a thing about Clifford. He used to say quite often that it was a source of wonderment that he, being what he was, had already lived nearly twice as long as someone like that, someone with so much jump and knowing in his horn, and so clean in his habits. That's the way, we said. Everything's yours, right in your hands, the whole deal, then it's yanked and nothing.

And we talked of what impossible hurricane of luck might blow us clear to Guatemala or Belize, somewhere warm at least, and how we would live there rich a long time like real human beings if we could, and enjoy the rain even, and be gracious toward everyone. Then we drank some more, and the horns welled and we were quiet.

It was probably about then I noticed the old people. They were some kind of couple and they were dancing, I guess. He was still tall and she never was, so he had to stoop to keep her his and gathered. The music was just junk but they liked it enough. They were both thin as pipes and the bones of his shoulders when he moved shrugged pegs through his suit. They picked up the pace, they swanked and juddered, and she held on her best.

Chummy by this time was blinking. He made a fist on the table, placed his head on it, and nodded out. I let him go and watched the old people again.

Jesus, they were ancient, and the strobes were merciless, badging them unearthly with reds and purples, and a very mean slash of yellow. But they were spry too, like they'd just been dug up and were hungry and they were meat to each other. They had the floor to themselves but were only using a foot of it. Then they kissed and kept at it. They were glued and feeding, working their jaws like pumps.

It was gruesome, I suppose, and it might have been disgusting. What made it amazing was, when they broke away for breath, there was a long loop of spit that drew out between them. It hung swaying from their chins and stayed with them as they danced, as they shut their eyes and danced, oblivious and serene inside their own scrap of forever. That's what knocked me out.

Chummy by that time had roused, and was humming or mumbling into his hand. "Chummy," I said, "you think you'll love me when we're old?"

He reared then. There was no blinking, and he seemed actually to focus, heaving his whole proud landscape of a face across the table into mine. "I don't even love you now, man."

He was probably lying, just trying it out for the sound.

"Well maybe you'll learn," I said. "Maybe you'll learn, my man."

Then we laughed, because we knew we'd never, absolutely never, have to put it to the test.

Scherzo

He had his beer, she had her dancing. He died. She didn't, not for a long time. When she did, she was already dead.

These were my parents. I never saw them. The night that gave me birth left me blind.

Even the void has its features.

We lived at Ram's End, amid the tumuli of slagheaps. Crows skraeled. Trains hammered by. The air was sulphur. I was told it was yellow. My father used his shoe for a fist. He went down the mine. A black wind blew. They brought him up for two days. She needed someone to hang on to. I was nine.

※

Life is unkind. I said that much later. She could not hear me then.

It rained in her room. Dogs ran the halls. She was poisoned daily. Cancer was a man in a suit. She spoke of cattle and lairage. I played the piano. In spoons, doorknobs, she saw the burning face of God. She heard the closet suffer. I found the drowned mice. Reeking of memory, she listened while I played. What is it like?, she managed. I continued to play. Tenderness gripped her. I felt it beat her, a pure ravishment. I continued to play.

Human will requires only the proper chisel.

❄

Göderich is a fidget. I calmed him. Tzgleti mocked me. I broke his code. Affliction was the ally. It let me despise.

I came of age. My fingers trapped a world. I mastered the false prophets, the martyr's blandishments. I entered the provinces of foreign skin.

I had her committed.

They let her out. She found me. I decamped, she found me. I surrendered.

There were lucid bouts. Meat arrived, fully cooked. She danced without falling. She did not drink dirt. The farce was brief. We became each other's bruise.

❄

A stylus scratched a record. It was sleet. Silence is a lie.

We lived in a barbarous city, above thieves and fools. No stars could be seen, I was told. She hoarded the food she stole from herself. She never went out. The excuse was winter. I forced her. Always she returned. I had the patience of an insect. My studies were vast and complex. I had touched the mystery. Someday I would strip it.

Of the rest I remember little, and quite enough. Plates fleered, shadows stalked. Assassins plotted in the pipes. A spider was my father. There, at least, I knew the satisfaction of a shoe.

She would live forever.

A barge of years passed. Frost got in. She bent, a misdriven nail. Her breath luffed. Teeth dropped. Combs broke through briar. Her dances shook her. More often, she collapsed. She had to be trundled then, a sack of onions, wherever the sun crawled.

Providence is a spiral. Belief is unnecessary. One has only to survive.

The house is high. We slept at the top. The walls are vellum, the stairs narrow and steep. A gate blocked them. I had it put in. A spasm of pity, long ago. She revelled to perch there, screaming down.

My studies had reached a critical stage. She sensed this. Her demands became monstrous. The words themselves were soot. Yet the antique machine scraped and boomed. It was a flogging, having to listen. There was no respite.

Failure dared my studies. Dread drained my hands. They warped. The piano was my enemy. It had come to that. I destroyed it.

Then I slept the last night.

Morning is always odious. The eager birds. Their sharp, pointless cries woke me.

But the incessant rasp was absent. I reflected a moment, then broached her room. I slapped the bed thoroughly. I kicked through the rubbish. Some dresses were torn. I regained myself.

Premonition is not proof. To search the house would mean half a day.

I began. The house was never so large. I was fortunate. Near the bottom of the stairs I nudged her with my foot. I had not locked the gate latch. Her attitude left no doubt.

We had a sane chat at last.

Between inner and outer dark there is peace.

My hands have forgiven me, and I them.

The new piano is superb, high spirited, a horse to be tamed. And yet how gentle is the mystery with me. I am serene. I can almost see it.

Sandcastles

They were boys running, three young boys with no place they had to be because they were there already, running on the beach with the summer inside them. The thin ones were brothers and the heavy one their friend, and as they ran he lagged, but they were all together, slapping their feet on the sand and kicking through the surf flashed by the sun. It was cider light, stronger than usual. Yet the sky was low, and held a drape of smolder, for there was always haze. Most days it didn't burn, staying heavy like grey wool and everything was vague. Today it was sparse, the wool pulled to gauze, and the sun came warm on their backs, their faces, on the new brown of their bodies, theirs to use.

The part of the beach where they were was crescent-shaped with a bluff behind, so it har-boured the wind and enlarged it. But there wasn't much now, only weak lifts from the sea. They spread their arms and held them, and when the breeze caught they became gulls anyway, fierce ebullient gulls with the throats of boys snatching the air fresh alive in their mouths. They climbed, stunted, soared. They scanned and drifted, and they swooped the pipers to see them skip. One of the boys roared and banked. He returned a plane, a fighter pilot in a spindle plane with blazing wings, so the others were, too, and they fought their shadows until each where they crossed crashed laughing down, and lay dead on the dunes.

Waiting for their breath they counted the waves – spools rolling, unrolling, long white furls like shavings, cresting and falling apart, gathering agaih – then forgot the waves and leapt up, roamed. Away from the shore, up where the banks curved and cliffed out, there was slashgrass that hid nests sometimes, so there might be eggs. They went there looking, poking around. One plucked a tine of the grass and blew a squall between his thumbs. Don't cut your lips, called another, pursing his like their mother. The brother blew louder, laughed.

They jumbled back to the shore, sailed stones and hunted shells. Dogwhelks and mussels, nothing good. Then suddenly a rare one, a fist-size spiral with a pink mouth. Glassy and cool, they held it to their ears, each other's ears to share the sea there, hear it surge in them and deepen. That was fine. After, they put it down carefully, and paced back steps like duelists, turned, and smashed it with rocks. Then, because there was no one to scold them no, they stared at the sun, seeing who could the longest. When they shut their eyes other suns appeared, and pinwheels with comet tails glittering back and forth in the black.

The heavy one got a stick, leaned on it and tottered about tapping, his eyes closed and feeling the air with his hand. He said he was blind, he was old and blind now, and please would they show him to the hospital? The brothers snorted and hooted, he looked so funny with his big legs in shorts and his shaky cane. They snapped to his side and led him about, up and down the beach. When they tired of that they said they'd arrived, the nurses could have him and stick him full of needles. They poked him and tried to trip him, at first, but he wouldn't, so they spun him instead. The brothers cried faster and he whirled, whirled round and faster round till the beach did with him, and they let him go. He staggered, a drunk old man, and toppled to his knees. He was happy on his knees, very happy but a little ill, and he dove his hands in the sand to still it.

It was then he saw something odd. When the sun stopped banging and he could balance, he crawled over and fished it out. It was a record, an old 45. It wasn't broken, hardly scratched. He showed it to the brothers. One side was "Cattle

Drive Blues," and the other had the title inked out. They didn't know who the singer was, but they admired the picture of a guitar, laid against the full face of a moon, with some tiny notes floating up. Each note had a cowboy hat. One of the brothers said that meant it was country music, which was mostly yodeling. They all tried a few howls until it hurt. Then the brothers wanted to skim the record on the waves, but the heavy one said no, it was his because he'd found it, and he was going to keep it. He put it on his head for a hat and walked. It wouldn't stay, so that was nothing. He turned it in his hands instead and made it a wheel, and they were off, with him in the lead now, driving where he would, his cargo of friends chuffing engines behind him.

When they rounded the narrow of the shore, down by the big rocks where the spray hit and the beach opened again, they saw ahead a bright tent pitched low on the sand. They held the horn loud and long. The tent moved. It unbent and stood, and the tent was a man. He saw them and waved. The beach was ruined a bit then. They let go of the train and plodded up aimless to where he was. When they got there, though, it wasn't a man anymore. It was a woman now, a short round woman in a huge sundress spatted with red dots like measles. She wore rubber boots, and was very pale and had a long fat neck. Black bangs made her face small, and when she spoke she notched her head aside like a bird asleep.

"Hello, boys," she said. "Now this is a surprise. I thought it was just me."

They said hello back and, no longer disappointed, looked at her, and at the records in her hand. She saw the guitar.

"I see you've found my music already. That was fast. Don't worry, you can keep it. There's more in the bag." She nodded her head. "It's good music."

The woman asked did they want to help her bury them, she had so many, and if they did they could get them from the bag. They each got an armful and clustered round. She laboured herself down and showed them how. "You just scoop a hole," she said. "Not too deep, just a little one." She dug with one hand, like a cat. "Then you lay the music in like this and then, then you put the sand back." It was only a sift she put over, so the record was barely hid, but she patted it and stood.

"There." She smiled and brushed her hands on her dress. "Now you can choose the place, boys, that doesn't matter to me. Anywhere's good. So long as the holes aren't too deep. I don't want them deep, that's the only rule. And you there," she added to the heavy boy, "you don't need to bury that one if you don't want. You can, but you don't have to. It's found already."

It didn't take long, not with the four of them, and the boys racing. The woman didn't move much, just stayed where she was and took her time, burying the few she had and the bag with the last. When they had them all in and covered, all but the one, she told them it was good what they'd done, that they were fine buriers. But she was tired now and they should have a seat some-place. There was a drift log by the water, good-sized and dry, and the four of them went there and sat in a row.

"Well," said the woman. "Here we are." No-body said much else for a while, then the shorter of the brothers thought to ask what her name was.

"I haven't got one," the woman said. "Do you?"

"Yeah," he said, but he didn't want to tell it now. He grinned and felt odd and looked at his feet.

"His name is Paul," his brother said. "Every-body's got a name."

The woman gave no sign she understood. He tried again slower, as though it were a compli-cated thing he should explain to her. "His name is Paul. And I'm Henry. We're related, we're broth-ers. I'm the oldest. And that's Phil there. His par-ents left him with us for the summer. We're Henry, Paul and Phil. See? Everybody's got a name. You have to have one if you're born."

"Well, I don't have one," she said. Then she leaned her neck out and through her hair asked sidelong down the log, "Why did your parents leave you, Phil?"

Too startled not to, he told the truth. "I don't know."

"Oooh," said the woman. "It's bad not to know. I wouldn't want that for me." She squinted at the three as though they were new to her now. Then she looked at Phil.

"You're a good boy. Sure you are, plain as day. Your parents must know it, they have to. And they'll remember, Phil, and come back. Why wouldn't they? Wherever they are, they'll come back like they said. Both of them will when they should, they'll find you and then, then it will all be the same. That's what they'll do. I know. They have to, Phil. You're a good boy, aren't you?"

There was nothing now but for him to admit he was, and to be embarrassed, and doubt everything again. But the woman seemed relieved. "That's fine," she said. "I was worried, but that's fine."

She began to rock a little and move the log, so the boys rocked with her. They heaved it for a horse until Phil, to be funny again, bucked backwards off. Something snapped. The brothers laughed, and the woman with them. Phil did too, though he was sorry in a way, because the snap was the record he'd fallen on. He reached under and showed it in two.

"Won't play now," he said. They laughed again and shaped palm-prints around him in the sand. Hers were large and uneven, and as she made them her arms, although it was only warm, gleamed their length and the underskin swung.

"Fleur-de-lys," she said, when they were done.

Phil got up and brushed his shorts and they watched the waves for a while, the low shrugs close in and the sweeps beyond that merged and lay flat. Some were combers, the woman told, and some others were breakers. She didn't know which, but they came from England, where the queen lived, the lady on the money. She had servants and lived in a castle, a hundred castles, hers to choose. "And there she is now," said the woman, pointing at where a seabird sat, far out, jouncing on the swells.

Soon as she spoke the queenbird flew, a slow kiting arc, and dwindled toward England. They waved. Then Henry saw a starfish with an arm gone. He fetched it to the log and they all felt the ridges and smelled the sea still a part of it. The woman tipped her tongue to the stub.

"Salt," she said, and put the starfish in her pocket. She looked around, shifted, and looked out at the sea. "Isn't it friendly?" she said, "rocking in like that?" Phil said yes, but Henry said no, it was cold. "You think?" said the woman. "I don't think so."

She asked a lot of questions after that. Did they watch the news, because she didn't anymore, not since it turned so ugly, but maybe they did? And when they went to bed did they sleep right away, or did they have to wait? Had they ever been lost? She had, when she was small. No one found her for a day. And did they know there's more germs in a human mouth, in theirs right now, than in any kind of a dog's? She had a beagle once but it barked all the time, so she had to give it up. But that was better, wasn't it, for a dog to be given away to a farm with wide fields where it could bark all the time and run around and no one minds it, wasn't that better?

Everyone agreed it was. A dog needed a place to chase things, rabbits and field mice, and bark when it wanted to. "Yes," she said. "I did the best there, all I could." She paused, and seemed to consider whether it was true. "The man who took him, the farmer, he came up from the mainland. He wore a tie." Then she wanted to know, did they ever think that the earth should be flat? That if it wasn't round, but smooth and flat like a table, you could go where it stopped, and stay there if you wanted, at the end of the world, just looking at it. "I'd like that," she said, "everything flat, so you could see it stopped."

"You'd fall off," said Henry.

"Yeah," she said. "Maybe I would."

The angle of the sun had moved higher and the breeze with it had knotted and turned, was thicker now, scuffling the crests and scooping in where they were. "It's windy and then it isn't," she said. "You can't ever tell."

She began to hum, not a song, only high, with a huff between like she'd lost a breath. Then, as though she hadn't been odd, she stopped, and had them guess how many dots there were on her dress.

It was Phil who was closest. "You've got the eye," she said. "There's six hundred and sixty-five. That's how many every time."

"That's a lot," said Henry.

"It's too many," said the woman. "I'm glad it's not one more." She looked down at her dress, at herself inside. "None of it's me," she said. The boys waited for the rest, for her to tell what she meant. But whatever she said they couldn't hear because her head was down by her knees, a string of hair in her mouth.

While she was there, Paul, pleased to think of it, announced, "Our cat's now got a name. She's Maeve. Our mother named her. She's white and she's got six toes." He searched for what else there was. "We had to drown her kittens. We didn't want to. They were nice. We had to." He let that settle. "It wasn't me that done it."

Now it was said, everything. He had told what he knew about names.

"She don't want to hear that," Henry said. Then, because he wasn't sure, he turned his voice as old and rigid as he could. "You're just stupid."

Paul stared at his feet again and kicked a strand of seaweed.

The woman didn't notice. Her head was still down and she was rubbing her legs, her palms and the back of her hands flipping along her thighs, stroking and smoothing, and plucking some. "How come you're —" started Henry, but abruptly she stood and went down to where the water was, spreading in and shawling away. She let it wash her boots, and looked out at the waves, and farther out to where they came from. The sun was behind the clouds and it was gull-colour out there, with ragged bands of grey across the rim fastened to the clear. She raised her arms and hung them out. Then she laid her hands on her face and left them.

It was then that the sun came back, bright, the strongest it had been. It sparked the waves sharp and made them hard. Then it shone through her dress and showed her skin, her panties that were blue like black and how fat she was, stark there to their eyes now and the red hover of the dots loose about and flowing.

There was no fault in this that was theirs, but they knew it wasn't right to see, to want to. They were shamed. They stared. Then Henry started to laugh, so Paul did too. They stopped when Phil shook his head and frowned, tapping at his cheek to tell them without saying that she was crying. It was true. She was crying in her hands, they could see that now. She was an adult crying because the sound was swallowed and her shoulders moved. She stayed that way, her back to the boys, and they, because they couldn't not, watched her stay, and waited for what would happen.

When she turned to them, there were finger marks on her face. More cloud had come by and broken the light, but she was smiling. "You can call me Maeve, too," she said. "That's a pretty name." She stretched her neck and cocked it. "Maeve. Don't you like it for me?"

With that she clapped her hands and came splashing out of the water, clapped again and sped her voice. "Boys," she said, "now I'll tell you what. Come down here and let's play a game. We'll play it and you can go. That's what we'll do."

"What kind of a game?" said Paul.

"It's a special game. It's called Sandcastles."

"We don't have pails," said Henry. "We'd need pails for the sand." He was tired of having to explain things. "That's for babies anyway."

"No it's not," she said. "It's for everyone. And we don't need pails. I'll show you. Now the first thing is, I have to lie down." She looked around, chose a spot without rocks, a few feet back of the water, and got herself down. She laid her head back on the sand, and straightened her legs out, as though she were lying at attention, then crossed her arms on her chest. "I'm ready," she said.

Then it was fun again burying the woman who was Maeve now. They got on their knees around her and dug at the sand, shoving it into banks and loading it on her; and they made cups with their hands and poured, enjoying the feel of it sieved through their fingers, dripping the sift on her thighs and belly and down her legs. She didn't say much, or move, only now and then lifted her head a little to watch and tell them they should use the dry sand if they could, but it didn't matter. When they had her covered they thought they were done, but she wanted it higher, so she couldn't see over to the sea, just look at the sky and watch the clouds.

Phil said about the tide then. "It'll be over your head. There's the mark, back there." He pointed where she couldn't see.

"Yeah. You'll get wet," said Paul.

"That's all right," she said.

So they piled it higher, until more sand than they put on ran off and she was just a head, and she said they could stop. She thanked them and told them she was tired.

"You can go now, boys. Go along, go home." She said it small and hollow, as from a well. They moved away some, but they didn't go. She was no one who could make them. They went up to the log and hung around but there wasn't anything to do there now, only stare at the mound and the woman under, at the blind back of her head on the sand like a black stone. Then they heard her call, snappish this time.

"Go away. I know you're there. Go away. You hear me? Clear off. "

"We should go," said Paul, looking to his brother for assurance. Henry shrugged and, not wanting to be the one to decide, picked up a rock. He thought to throw it the sea. But she was there and she'd hear it hit, and say something. He tossed it by the log instead.

"I guess," he said at last. "She knows about the mark."

"She's gonna get wet," said Paul.

But Phil said, "Wait." He left the log and, stepping carefully on his shadow stretched long and thin in front of him, went down to the mound.

He stood by her head. There was sand on her cheek, and through her hair. A line in her forehead twitched.

"Do you want us to tell?" he said.

She didn't answer. The sun was direct above and shone on her face. He put his hand across to shield. Nothing moved in her face except the twitch and the dark his hand made. He held it there, opening and closing his fingers, barring the light and slatting it through. He played at that, sliding shadows across and changing her face that didn't change, that stayed shut like a door. Then he dropped his hand and tried once more.

"Maeve. Do you want us to tell?"

She opened her eyes and looked up, straight into the bright and the round far-away face that mooned down at hers. "I don't know," she said. Then she closed her eyes and the door shut again.

He was banished now. It had happened again. It felt like falling. He didn't know why, but he could feel that it was true. And then he understood. There was nothing to do, nothing at all they had to, and there never had been. It didn't matter if they told, or if they didn't. It was only a game not for them, something adult and strange, and it was over now.

He turned away and went back to the log. The brothers were as they were, where he'd left them, standing around and waiting for what was next, for him to tell them. He was silent. They stood a moment, another. They looked at him, and he at them. No one looked at the mound. He knew what they didn't and that was his to keep. He waited more. The waves lapped, yet everything was still. Then one started to run, slow at first then fast as he could, so the others did too. They followed and overtook, ran beside, beyond. The beach was theirs now. It was theirs alone and they were boys again, three young boys together and apart, racing carelessly toward home.

Before You Were Born

It's handed down, I guess, what all you might die for and never know why, maybe kill for too, but I know for sure they didn't have a clue what they were in for, this young couple, and they weren't even that then, just two strays flung together on a couch, in his father's basement, the proud dumb sounds of a party slamming through the floor —

because the boy down there, and that's what he was despite his size and the lock-knife he liked to carry, this inward useless boy alive inside her like never before, he had an older brother upstairs, a flat-top army sap now, shipping next week for some tribal place that no one laughing the house apart then, not the brother or the father or the gearhead friends, could tell from hell on a map, or spell it either —

and he didn't care himself, because the girl on the couch, this beautiful creature stuck to him moving, hands flying and her hair in his mouth, she was one of those marked ones, he'd seen it from the start like a shine on her, that she would chase and chase and keep on chasing blind until she found the first ambush she was raised to fall for, and he meant to be it—

except he needed a lure, he thought that way then and was probably right, there wasn't much his own to brag on but an old count for smashing street lights Halloween night and shoplifting twice, kid stuff, but if he kept that up he'd be turning lathe soon enough, and he'd skipped school so many times going back was no option, so he was clamped where he was, pumping weights in the basement and running a car he couldn't quite pay for, a shit-box Vette with a shot transmission that pissed oil, and three or four nights a week in a hairnet he swung a dead shift for the minimum and day-old cake in the sour heat of a Swedish bakery, thinking the whole time how far her backbone bent—

and she, well, there was another guy, a senior-year athlete come from money who could play the trumpet and had an easy way, apparently, of getting her to forget what she wanted to, because while her mother didn't whore it exactly, she was most-way there, and that good office job next week, well, it stayed next week, that's the way it was, so when the banker's son was busy or whatever and they did get together, a drive or a movie, there was all that freight in her head and he couldn't just relax and glide, he had to search the right words and try to lift it with her —

but what did he know of how that was done?, his own mother fled before memory almost, and his father hardly spoke and not at all of her, except the odd month when the body shop laid him off and he was sipping from a hip flask and got that split rock grin, and with his brother, well, it was like a contest who could be harder, always had been, although now he was leaving some truce had been struck, and he'd wished him good luck and said duck your head, that kind of thing, and they even shook hands, it was just burning the trash but right to do —

a couple months dragged, back and forth from the bakery, same stall with the girl going nowhere clear, then everything snapped, inside and out, all the little he knew changed and began to rush, first thing happened was his brother's patrol ran over a landmine and he came home in a plane from Afghanistan, everyone knew where it was by then, and they had to herd in line to see him, this hero, except they couldn't because the casket was shut, flag-draped and his picture on top, same straight-on cropped one the papers used and his father razored out and pasted on the fridge, half a dozen blunt ghost faces that could have been his, should have been maybe —

then a day right after when he was under the Vette in the driveway frigging break pads his father staggered from the house and stood over him mumbling, so he slid out from under and faced him, and then his father said it plain who should be living, and gave him the reason he'd been waiting for always and he knocked him down, and when he sprang up like a recoil he knocked him down again, and wasn't sorry any-more, not for nothing in the world, it felt that good —

then he got some more luck, because the mother of the girl it happened she went for a stroll and bounced down a stairwell and came to in the emergency, that's how they told it, the mother and the long-haul driver they lived with then, this rehab reject who went after her with a bat, one of those fat plastic kid's bats so he had to work at it, and the doctor for some reason accepted the sleepwalk story, so the girl when she could, well, she made the next move —

he was living at this time in a sort of concrete bunker across from a racetrack, they used to store horse feed in there or something, sharing it with a dealer who went by Gary D., a cord-thin smart guy with B.B. eyes only a fool would trust, yet there were plenty of those going so they made out fine, and his own job was simple, sharp eyes and muscle, applied as needed, so when there came a rap at the door that didn't stop he slapped the bolts open with a wrecking bar in his hand, but it was only her, her alone in the rain standing with a knapsack and asking could she stay, a few days, a week—

they spent their first full night together on the floor, a torn mattress and a six of warm beer, listening to the rain club the roof, and planning, planning a lot, and by morning they had it figured, because Gary D. wasn't so smart after all, leaving them there like that, this young couple with nothing to lose, they saw their best chance and took it, the drugs and Gary's extra gun, and they ran—

he was eighteen, she was sixteen soon, and it was real heaven at first, he would hot-wire cars and siphon gas and sell some coke here and there and buy a load of pills and sell those, and they were sleeping in motels with cable TV and eating Chinese every night, he got a snake tattoo that wrapped his wrist and she let her hair whip loose and sat on his lap in a mall booth that flashed their picture four times, all different, and he knew without looking he was someone else, and he gave her a heart bracelet with their names cut in and they traded vows they made up, and some of them held for a while—

then he sold the last coke and rolled a drunk for two-fifty and a watch he pawned but they burned through that, and there were things to fight about they hadn't thought of before, because the more he stole the more they needed, they were eating pills by the bag, feeling sick and his hands twitched, hell, most of him shook and she went skinny as a stick, so it came down to begging and sleeping in a park, but he wouldn't let her trick, he drew the line there and felt proud almost, and then a crazy lady with a hairless pug that looked like a pig gave them forty dollars if they'd accept Jesus, and they tried hard a few hours to use some of it different, ice cream and pinball, their feet in a wading pool as the sun snuck across, pretending in the shimmer life could look like that—

but between them still clung a strong sort of static like the air before a storm, and one night in an alley behind a bar it burst and he hit her, this beautiful creature, and broke her nose, and she bled all over into his hair as he grabbed her waist to him and dropped to his knees on the glass, and stayed there pleading until she had to believe him, because she didn't have a choice, she was racked on speed and pregnant then and they loved each other still, there was no help for that, but they didn't know how so they thought it was hate, and it ground on like it was, but not for long—

because this hopeless man decided it would stop, one way or another, so he said some lie to make her stay behind and walked away straight into a bank, wearing a ski mask and pointing the gun that five minutes later wasn't his anymore, he was knee-pinned to the floor with a muzzle at his skull, and he got six years, they said he was lucky, and he had to agree because she showed at sentence day, and the last thing he saw, there were tears, real tears—

now that was last year and nothing has changed I know of, so I guess that's why I'm writing you this, wherever you are, and I hope when you can read someone lets you have it so you can know at least where you came from, and maybe, later on, you could try to find us and forgive us for it, maybe you could do that, later on.

Your loving father

Tell

I

Tom Sydney wasn't a natural – he had to learn to lie. The usual reason.

Blonde, in leotards, his daughter sat beside him. It was Tuesday, dance day, and he was driving her. The school was an old church, rechristened Pegasus. Hordes attended, every child graduated. The recitals were endless. There was never enough parking.

He said what he always said, and dropped her out front. She bounced inside. Her classes lasted an hour and a quarter. He had time for a haircut.

He took the back way, an extra five minutes. Oaks, maples, stone houses from another century with lawns smooth as pool tables. It was a gracious town, expensive, a bit dull. He had grown up there. He went by the Barbatos' place.

The cabin cruiser was in the driveway, showing its age. SeaRovers did that. Mr. B. might go for an upgrade.

Another block and he saw a dog with an odd gait, lunging through the spray of a sprinkler. It had only three legs, but didn't seem to know it. It made him think – he couldn't help it – of his daughter: her talent, certain at eight, wavered at nine, had become a mirage at ten. She was eleven now. Polite, gregarious, bearing a slight paunch, she still loved herself in mirrors. He still kissed her goodnight. He was thinking about that – what difference, if any, proper balance might have made – when, at a yellow light, he stalled the car. No one honked, but he felt foolish, and wronged somehow.

Then his wife called, which she rarely did. Just saying hello between clients. Claire was a physiotherapist; she kneaded people. They had often laughed about that. Tom was a salesman of high-end boats and accessories. That was funny, too, because under certain conditions he had a small fear of water. Not that it showed; even Claire didn't know, and now, after fifteen years, he certainly couldn't tell her.

Janet knew. It had drawn her to him, his confession at the marina, over drinks. (He wasn't looking. She could have been a buyer.) That's sweet, she'd said. He agreed, and risked her knee.

Smartly dressed, more compact than slender, she was shorter than he was, and that was nice. She had an open, winning manner, easy to be with. Neither husband had understood this. The first, a musician who had gone nowhere, was, although attractive, grasping and critical, and they had nothing in common. The second was Bob McLean. Tom knew him, everyone did: his face was on half the construction projects in town. He was clever and lucky, in about equal measure, but ungenerous, and not so attractive. The comb-over alone, she said, was sufficient grounds. She kept his name, and a decent settle-ment.

He was meeting her tomorrow. Her place, the penthouse. They would have the afternoon, the view, some wine. It was flawless. And she pos-sessed, when she wished, an insinuating voice. A little riven, grainy, like a broadcast from the twenties. It took him places he had never been, but recognized when he got there.

The guilt was tidal – it came and went, and had its own channel, off to the side. What spilled over he was dealing with and, in a practical way that surprised him, it had gotten simpler, almost normal, yet better than that. He was more atten-tive at home, more romantic. Janet's building had some shops, including a florist's. On his way out he would stop and buy a rose.

It was his first affair, and Tom would never be a veteran. He couldn't do that to Claire, they shared too much. What he had with Janet was something else, sweeter, but not deep. When it would end, or why, was beyond him. Something small would change, for him or for her. Neither would deny it. She would not forget. He would not look back. He knew his limits.

The back route had been a mistake. A closed lane, sewer construction, and, before he saw the signs, he was locked in. By the time he got loose he knew he was going to end up being late getting back to his daughter, and that bothered him.

He caught a break at the barber shop. Gus had a customer, but the far chair was free. Tom waved and slid in. The other barber was new, and bent over with a whisk. There was a lot of hair on the floor and he was getting it all. Tom looked at the clock, and looked at Gus. Gus shrugged, and kept snipping. His guy was thin, with sideburns. They were nearly finished. Tom looked in the mirror at himself. He hadn't changed much since college. A little pouchy, but that was his mother in him, and he still had the strong jaw.

His ears weren't level, though. (He hadn't seen that until Janet told him not to worry about it.) The other guy had a diamond in one of his

ears. Did that mean he was gay? – he had a
leather jacket – or was he just trying to be young?
Gus was brushing off his neck now. The guy paid
and left. Tom noticed that he didn't leave a tip.

The new barber had washed his hands, thor-
ough as a surgeon, and was ready. Just a trim,
Tom told him, I'm in kind of a rush.

II

Multiplied in a sun-struck series of shop windows, Stuart Roöp's image gave the impression
he was racing himself, and that was true. He had
a song in his head. There were fifty-plus in a box
he kept in the closet, and the same again under
his bed. This one came from there.

The lead singer loved it. He had said as much
in the Gents, while relieving himself. The problem was the bridge. It was too tricky for the Sons
of Oblivion. No guarantee, but if he chopped the
bridge and most of the lyrics, six minutes could
be made into three, and it could work. They
would have to change the title, add the feedback,
put their names in the credits. Simple as that, said
the singer – a deaf person could dance to it.

That was yesterday. The Sons were rolling out
Thursday morning. He had been up when the

sky turned blue, and might be again tomorrow. The bridge was crucial, and the key rhymes involved the title, so he just didn't know. He went for a walk, he needed a haircut anyway. Walking would help him relax.

It didn't work. At Gus's a man with a fake smile, impatient, came in. A sales type with some big deal he had to get back to. He drummed his fingers, sighed, and he kept glancing over. Stuart saw his eyes in the mirror. Small and quick in a round face. He didn't look gay, but you never know. He was glad when Gus finally finished his neck so he could pay and get out of there.

He was headed home now. A basement apartment, and not that clean. She never made an issue of it. They got together every other Wednesday; yoga was the cover. She had a long nose, glasses, and legs like a springbok. Freckles on her breasts. Simple tastes: Kahlua, baby oil. She liked to be naked, and often spoke of her daughter, who was artistic and, partly because of that, immature. It was, all in all, satisfying rather than urgent, and he assumed she felt the same way.

They had met at the White Horse. He subbed at the bar, ran sound checks. Sometimes he played, though not often now. That night he was. He remembered that it was Ladies' Night, two-for-one margaritas, and that it was someone's birthday. The teenage hilarity, the big gestures – you can always tell.

She wasn't on the make, and she hated deception. She confided that later, and he believed her, as far as it went. She was too literal for that and, it was true, when not in bed, she was inclined toward vacancy. You didn't notice right away, and it went with the job, he supposed. She was a physio, she kneaded people. It was her only joke. Someone must have taught it to her.

Her husband was the guy you hear about. Solid as a brick, the weekly rose. He took out the trash and played a lot of golf at private clubs, for the contacts. He sold yachts, and he was terrified of water.

Claire's attitude toward this was mixed; she thought it was a laugh that he tried so hard to conceal something so trivial, when it was obvious anyway, and she seemed disappointed that he did such a poor job at hiding it. She had him coming and going, it seemed, on prongs. It was more than Stuart wanted to hear, and he felt a wince of sympathy.

His own wife, when he'd had one, briefly, was forever misprising him. She thought he was unusual, irresponsible, spontaneous, a typical musician. It was why she married him, and also why she left. In fact, although he was not aware of it then and could never abide it now, he had wanted little more than that which she appeared to offer: the refuge of a tolerant order. Sure, he smoked a little dope, who didn't then? His friends weren't hers, and hers he didn't like, except one. And he did give her the wrong Valentine, but they got over that. It didn't amount to much, his sins. He knew guys who did heroin, and the drummer in the band had robbed a convenience store.

Janet didn't see it that way. He got a tip on a horse one time, long odds. On a lark he bet, and won, two months' rent. He thought he was vindicated, he had earned a gift. It turned out he was just the cat you put up with, dropping a mouse at the door. They were young, of course, or he was, anyway. Janet was different, twenty-five with the heart of a judge. She'd have made a good mother.

He would have to cancel Wednesday and didn't want to tell Claire. She could hardly blame him, and wouldn't. His reluctance to call her was absurd, he knew that. Yet he didn't expect to be believed. It was something in his manner, his voice, a diffidence so practiced it had stiffened into reflex, and seemed natural. People thought he was lying when he wasn't. When he was, they believed him. That could be a good quality, in a song.

His heart wasn't in it, that was the trouble. He was pushing forty. If this one didn't open, how many more doors would there be? Or maybe the singer was having him on, it wouldn't be the first time. He didn't like to think about that, but it wouldn't be unfair. Claire thought it was their song, written for her. He regretted that, but it was the least of his worries. He had come to care, but not that much. She had her own life and, whichever way it went, she was not likely to know.

III

In the shadow of the school, her back to the rough brick, Molly Sydney stood waiting. Everyone was gone, except the weird kid on the steps, playing jacks. No one talked to her, so Molly didn't either. For a while she had waited on the curb, but too many people drove past. They saw her in her dance suit, and smiled. When a brat in a safety seat pointed, she flipped him the finger.

It was too cool in the shade but she wasn't going to move. She would suffer, and he would know; she would tell him so for being late again, and for leaving her there, always the last one. She checked her watch. Another five and he would break his record. She hoped he did. She didn't care.

She shooed a bird from a piece of crust with her foot but it kept coming back. Then a man walked by in a hurry. He cut through the schoolyard, snapping his fingers. He was wearing a leather jacket, and he was as old as her dad. She hated that.

And she hated ballet. It was boring and her feet hurt and she wasn't good at it anymore. She wanted to quit. Her mom wouldn't mind. She didn't pay attention to much these days, not since she'd gotten into yoga. Her dad was different. *You can do it, Moll. Try a little harder.* He was always reaching. It was too much. She was almost twelve. She could wear her mother's shoes, and she knew girls with condoms in their knapsacks. Two boys in her class sold Valium.

Her parents were clueless. They thought her sitter Jade was so great. She was in high school, and she swore and smoked. Molly saw her behind the shed, when her boyfriend came over. She had to promise not to tell, but maybe she would. It wouldn't be lying, she had crossed her fingers. If she did tell, it would only be to her dad, and he would blame himself. He did that a lot, when it wasn't his fault. Then she'd bring up ballet.

He did break the record. He had the window down before the car stopped, apologizing. He didn't look sorry, he looked happy. He must have sold a boat. Getting in, Molly decided she wouldn't tell him, about anything, not today. She would save it. He was in too good a mood now. Tomorrow would be better. After his golf game, when he wasn't so cheerful.

Then Tom said what he always said, and he drove his daughter home.

Grebec

Early of a May morning the old man swiped the curtain and looked out at where it happened. He saw that it was spring.

The last flitch of snow had given up overnight, and the forsythia was back, the tight buds bright as bees and set to flare, and there in its branches, like a stashed piece of sky, preened the jay that had lured him, silent now. He yanked at the sash, yanked again and it gave. Drips off the eave pocked and slow woken flies batted about the pane. One whirred on his wrist, righted, crawled the bole of his knuckle – broke when Charlie Ross clipped it with the maul that time – and into his palm. He wiped it on the sill and kept looking, breathing the earth in the air and staring at the lawn, the scars and gouges, the hog wallow they rucked it into on that pit of a night when they drove on it wild, wailing the banshee.

A year ago now. Didn't seem so long, but in another way it did, as though his life right there had split in two and as one part went on, the other dragged. At the same time, neither was really moving.

He'd get to it today, start filling the ruts, the ground was loose enough, and he could see at the drive's end the mailpost listed more, so he'd straighten that too, because there might be a letter from the girls, they were each of them due. He'd stake it tonight, maybe he would, when he went for the bills and the other trash, as he did now from habit in the relief of the dark. Ever since the two times there was a bag stuffed in and a note he didn't read because the heft was shit and the notes would be no different.

It was all when he came back, just after. He didn't tell Cora about the bags, but she saw the sticks set up. Struck in the lawn, alongside the forsythia, the stark white cross like a slap he should have seen first to spare her that. He burned it in the stove and she cried, and he didn't know what to do when she went that way, never had.

October that was, leaves flying and the first flurries, soft as chick fluff. There was work to be at. Storm windows, and the sump had burned out. And the roof needed doing, some shingles. He had it most done, then getting up he stepped wrong. The ladder threw, he leaned to counter but it was going over and in a second he was scrabbling, hanging from the chimney strut.

Anyone could have seen, driven by and marked him shamed. He knew he'd drop, break his legs at least, but didn't somehow. He kicked and kneed and scrapehauled himself up and, arm-cords jumping, laid his length out of sight on the roof. He lay a good while, then finished the shingling.

He didn't tell Cora that either. She had enough to bear, what with the phoning then. Any hour, at supper or in the middle of the night, a man he didn't know, or a woman sometimes, her voice the worst, like a wasp in a bottle. If he let it ring it would a hundred times, louder the longer, and even when it wasn't them it seemed it was until he answered, so he turned the ringer off. No one called now.

Behind him the fire they wouldn't need much now ate a knot and hissed a scoot of blue flame. It wasn't low, but he went over to poke it and laid another log on, leaving the door inched for draft. Squatting there, the ache in his knee worked a blade beneath, and his back seemed a plank.

Spring would limber him, but he'd miss the fire, smoke in his clothes and chopping the wood, skimming it in on the pallet sled. It was something needful and he could go out to the barn, foxfoot those first weeks as though robbing his own place. He'd go split some wood and have a smoke then and be alone. He was tasting that when, from the kitchen flung down the hall to ferret him, came Cora's voice calling *Carl, you there? Carl?* Her odd strained voice that had been all their time so sweet to hear, a ruckle he'd told her, a dove – they were lying in bed with the Sunday sun, before the girls, that was; they were new-wed young and the loose of her hair in his hands shone, same as the sun, and his name in her mouth filled his – but what hit his ears now was a blackbird's bitter one.

He shook his head and sighed and, forbearing any sliver of the harshness she'd search for, sent back *yeah*, he was here, he hadn't stepped out. He was here where she knew he was and had to be, inside the house or about it not far, nowhere with people much. That suited him now; they'd turned their backs. The Bartons, Vaughans, and Margaret Ross, they'd turned. Hemphills of course, and the feed and hardware men the one time he went in shied like a quail covey, so the hell with them. Estes too. But he wouldn't have thought that of Spurge. They'd shared some times, and hadn't he gone over when the pied foal came twisted and they'd pulled together, slickthrust past their elbows with the mess of birthing, and blown into its nostrils his own breath until it startled and lived?

And the church. He didn't care about that, he'd had his fill of pews. Cora did, though, she minded, she'd lost the Auxiliary, teas and suppers and such and it was hard on her, the lack of that to go to, no dressing up and no one coming round.

There was Norman of course, he'd stood for him. But he couldn't drive, not since he put the pickup in the ditch. Gliding from the Legion, damn fool, in a snowstorm, too, and him with the eyepatch and all. He was a walking man now, except he couldn't walk, not far, so he'd called him a couple times and there was said a few things that needed saying. But Norman was part deaf and they had to shout, and they were never much for the phone anyway. So there was only Doris and Bill when they could, for an hour or so, and the grocery fellow, if that's what he was, his hair pulled behind and tied in a ribbon. None but them, and the fat man from town, every other Friday come to gape and pester, checking he hadn't fled yet. What did he think, where'd he guess he'd be, gone to Florida? Cora liked the visit, it was that for her, she could lay out biscuits and make the tea; she plumped the pillows and before he came she cleaned, wiping the corners. All for the fat man.

He knocked the stove door wide, spat into the fire, then clanked it shut and straightened in stages. He was weary, and he hadn't done a thing yet. Rusted lugs, he thought, and chuckling at that switched the ceiling fan to high and eased into the wingback under the lave shoved down. There was nothing beat wood heat.

But he'd been glad for the winter, the blunt days and long darknesses, and for the wind even, the clout of it, every night, it seemed, across the field singing the wires high and smacking the house. And glad too for the cold. Twenty, thirty below a fair stretch, never much over – ice beading the walls, and the pipes froze: he bathed them with the acetylene – but that was all right, winter stilled the world down and let him breathe. And the freezing cleared the sky and there'd be stars, the colder the more stars, always the Plough most called the Dipper and the Hunter's stud-belt, and over up the North Star's ingot his own father with an arm that touched it singled out, saying a hand's spread meant twenty degrees and a thumb was two, look there boy, see it and don't forget, so when you found the bright one, the lantern light, you couldn't be lost, yes, they'd be there, and the broadcast sparks of all the rest he'd forgot, outlasting anything done under them.

So when he went to the barn, breaking through the drifts to his hips heavy as feed sacks, the wind switching his face and he had to bang ice from the hasp, if it wasn't peace he felt then, it

was something near, an unweightening and loos-
ening, the shell of his age cracked and sloughed
as he drove the axe through the hardwood, good
dry maple and beech, cleaving the blocks neat
through the heart, he had the eye for that yet,
though his wind lacked, and splitting the kin-
dling finer than needed so he could keep there
longer, turn out the light and sit on the shed stool
in the calm absorption of the black, wind creak-
ing the beams and the mice ramping.

He'd listen to that and roll a smoke, because
Cora couldn't stand it in the house, not since it
happened and she changed, as everything had,
the solid breadth of the farm and him on it, the
wide feeling gone, and her bothered now by
what she'd never minded before, him smoking
some and any little sound she didn't know right
away, any silence either. The radio had to be on
and the television all day, filling the house,
every room with yammer and what was supposed to be music now, so it was the barn and
shed left. But the freedom of even that was less,
he couldn't be long out or she'd fret herself raw,
and when he came in he'd have to take it, that bit
between his teeth. He couldn't grudge her. There
were nights yet she'd wake moaning from the
dream they were back, waving the torch.

She'd be heated like a griddle then, and her
neck wet. He'd turn on the light, leave it on and

soothe at her, he owed her that. Not to be angry or show the hardness. But he'd warned them, how many times stood on the porch, shook his fist and warned them off, by god how many? They chunked rocks and broke the window out, two hundred for the new one, and hailed bottles on the roof, Cora trembling as they smashed. They did all that and laughed.

What choice did he have? It was stand or be driven, and thinking it even now he was gripping the armchair. Then the wall clock Cora hauled from a yard sale home clicked eight and the damned whatever it was trapped inside there started to bong. He pushed up from the chair and went back to the window. The jay was gone, and the flies. Nothing stirred except, across the road a quarter klik, the sun flashing Stott's roof and the chimney smoke going straight up. Yes, spring was late this year but here to stay, and Stott would be well on to shearing soon. Now that was a job, and he could have it, those oily old Shetland ewes reeking of wet rag.

Stott was alright, though. Bought the place after Dodge Murray dropped dead haying, switched it over to sheep, and made a go of it. And a day after New Year's Stott saw him shovelling and tromped over. They'd only spoke a few times, but he just wanted to say if he was him, maybe he'd of had to. That was it exact, and he was the only one, save Norman, the only soul in the whole of Grebec understood.

It made no sense. Grebec was a right place, always had been. It mattered whose well went dry, what was doing down the road. Where'd that go? Time was there were pound parties here and shivarees, and you could raise most of a barn in a day or two, everyone showed and pitched in. And when you went over it wasn't your ass on parade, some hospital, and strangers paid for the handling. Your own laid you out. After the washing you were shaved and dressed and they got you proper in the best room, parlour if you had one, so those who should could come and see and remember who you'd been all your life. The linen was clean, they half-dollared your eyes and there were candles lit, and they wrapped your jaw in a scarf like you needed to go out and it was storming there. They did it right in the old times. His mother had for his father when the oak he was felling kickshanked and he was under. The neighbour wives helped, he was seven then, and old enough, and John was nine and still alive before the typhoid. Mrs. Bates brought the candles with a rabbit stew and his mother thanked her and they ate, not looking at the head chair until his mother moved it. She lived on thirty years getting smaller, as though the sun that day had made its slip toward evening and she was the shadow of something tall going down slow.

Now they gut you quick like a beef cow and ship you off. A lot don't even get the ground, just bone and soot and thrown to the wind, that wouldn't be for him. He'd paid for the spot in the Allendale kirk, on a rise where an elm the Dutch blight hadn't got arched over, so there'd be green above and a mat of colour when the leaves fell. It was fine enough there but he'd rather it here, for himself on the farm if he could, maybe down by the pond where the bullfrogs twanged and deer came to drink in the cover of the alders, and wild-flowers fought the grass and ran like a fever, that'd be all right, but the law wouldn't let it. And there was Cora to think of. So he chose the knoll plot away from the road, in the back with the meadow view. He'd get the stones set soon, now it was spring, and give the carver their names and the two dates, he'd nick them in and leave the spaces after smooth for the rain to polish until the day that was his, because he'd be the first, he felt that for certain, he'd get in there ahead and warm the bed for her. Plenty folks used to say that and it was good to think of, tucked at the last like at the first, together.

There was that at least. And the farm. He smiled and ran his fingertips on the screen and, for no reason he knew, poked where it was torn and tore it more. The farm, sure, but how long? They could sell, he was mulling that, for Cora he was. It was always there, clung like a web astride the run of his mind, the queer dread thought of moving off. But who'd buy? What price would they get? When he auctioned the back acres, the baler and the tractors with it, the harrow and the rest, he'd sold high or he wouldn't have done it, and never would have if they'd had sons. Anyway, none of the young wanted a country place, it was too far from lights, and the old were too old. And if they did sell, where then? Into town, or some other town, a box somewhere stacked in a kennel of boxes? He couldn't take that.

But Cora, though. She'd went to her sister's when he was away and she should have stayed. They'd have let her, kin has to. She could have knit with Doris and had some chat and Bill would tease her. There'd have been better, or with one of the girls. Darla most like, she had the big house, but that was the prairie and Cora wouldn't leave him anyway. So she was here too, stuck with him on this shunned scrap of earth she hated now. Not that she'd say, but he knew her heart bare and he saw in it how she hated now. And him too, she must a little, in the beaten part of her. Because if he mentioned the land, any plans he might have, raise some chickens maybe, a few to keep his hand in, the hung look she got then, and in her eyes the farness, showed him plain it was no use anymore hoping what strangered her would pass and she'd be Cora again.

It was the trout pond settled it. He could smell it yet, seemed he could when the wind was fresh, the sweeted grab of the fumes when he went out that morning to feed them and they were belly-up floating in the rainbow colours of the gas, a hundred live fish dead because that was their pleasure, to ruin and waste. He called the Mounties again and they came, two with the leg stripes, down their backs more like, and he told them who did it, same as before, everyone knew. The Gibson boys, and Lucas Hemphill's son Cecil, the big lout he'd let ride the black horse way back when he wasn't big, only a gangly kid happy to be let ride, and the other one with them from the new family up the road, Ontario people he didn't know the name of then. He'd told them who it was, and that it had to be ended.

Didn't mean a thing, though, not a rat turd's worth. They just gawked at him blank and wrote it on a pad to forget it, because what did they know of him or Grebec and the way things were here, farming your guts out on the dry acres so they'd yield and make of yourself with it something fine to befit a man's labour in his life. And then, then no-counts, punks like these. That was allowed now, was it?

So to make them see, though it pained him, he said it was fifty years he'd worked this place, this forsaken ground right here under their feet redeemed all the way from those woods back, and a lot more besides, bucksawing the trees and busting stumps, half lost a finger in the chain once and cracked his knee when the tractor reared. Still he bulled at it, hiring extra when he could, cropping alone in the lean times, hauling rocks by the ton and breaking the brick clay over and again to richness. His doing. And he built the house, he told them that, too. Flush atop the stones of the old one, built it plumb to last and slung the porch around where Cora used to dangle in the swing chair, fanning while the chimes tinked, and the girls they'd raised played their games till they were married and away. All of his own sweat made, fifty years, more than fifty, and that wasn't nothing. But that was what they wanted, the four of them, to tear it down and make it nothing. Didn't anyone see that? Didn't they? And then he ran out of words.

One looked off at the sky, the other sucked his belly in and said they'd have a talk with the families and be around more, do what they could. Sure they would. They'd talk and talk and idle by blind and it would never be over.

The Mounties left. He watched them disappear, and stayed a little after, just looking at things. When he turned to the house it was him alone against the taking.

He kept it in the shed. Hadn't used it since the coons. Or before that, when the coy-dog staggered from the woods, broad daylight, crossed the field jakelegged and stopped, drooling, by the barn, snapping its jaws at nothing there. Not since then. He took his time with the rod, with the cloth and the oil, stroking it clean inside and out till the barrel shone like a trumpet, and the chasing and the breach gleamed, and the brass of the shells. He wrapped it in a horse blanket and stowed it by the porch door, in the wood box.

Cora was asleep. She'd taken the pills that gave her that, dropping her like a wader stepping off a ledge into deep water. He eased the door shut and went out. Then he laid the shotgun across his knees and waited, three nights on the porch in the swingchair, watching.

The first it rained, off and on, more mist than rain, and in the last slivers of burnish the air seemed to shimmer. He remembered that and how warm it was. On the second, the sky was a swollen bag that split in one rush. The roof rang, the gutter choked and flowed over. He watched the spout cascade, the rain strafe the rail and jump. It was past two when he went in. The third night he waited was starless, tar-black. A breeze flicked the chimes and it got late again. He had a thought to go in, he was bone-tired now and they weren't coming, not tonight.

Then they came.

The grope of the beamlights showed over the rise, the sky glowed, and then by the dive down and coming up again so fast, he knew it was them. They tore down the road and slewed into the drive, spun around and slammed onto the lawn and kept coming. But the ground was swamped and they were mired, gunning the tires. The eyes of the car stared straight at the porch, but he'd thought of that and was down, behind the swingchair crouched, riding the barrel on the little sway. They spilled out, stumbling and cursing each other, cursing him as though he was the dirt, him and not them, pig-drunk out front there on his own land, falling and getting up, then someone yelling they'd burn him out and laughing.

There was a blast of light. One of them waving a torch, that was all he could see, the flashloom of the shape huge by the forsythia, the loudest with the torch jerking it back and forth.

He fired quick twice, he remembered only one but they told him it was twice.

Bastard shouldn't have been standing. But he was, a shocked animal thing wearing the mask of a boy. Then the dark sap from its chest spread, and spread, and poured into the cup of hands too small to hold it, then took a step. One step, and seemed from the inside to melt, as though it had no bones. The torch guttered out, and toppled into the muck. The others ran. He heard the boots suck. It was dark and still. And the feeling then, god help him, the feeling then was the laden weight of a greed lifted and satisfied.

They took him cuffed.

The trial was short, a lot of butterfly talk. He had been afraid for his life, his lawyer said, and besides, he was old, too old to matter. So they let him go, he'd serve his sentence at home, waiting for the day that was waiting for him. He'd pluck the short straw, and that would be forever. But a moment then, if he had the luck, he'd see it for a gift, like the coy-dog did by the barn when it stood and it stared asking. He'd want that snap of time to know the rightness.

The old man shut the window, banging it down, and before he turned his name came again for him calling, Cora calling *Carl, breakfast's on, Carl*.

He knew she'd keep on, rasping that file, so he
started back to the kitchen, thinking on what he'd
say while they ate. She'd need him to chat, what
of didn't matter, something pleasant and useless
that would comfort her and be no part of him. So
he settled on the spring, yes, he'd give her that
before she asked. He'd tell her spring was here
now because the forsythia was, new-risen out
there where they could see it every year, every
day this time of year, young and yellow and soon
a fire of blooming.

Dalat by Night

It was a new country now, and that suited him. The hotel had a bar on the roof, well above the smog. Palms, white linen, a calm, forgetful aura. He spent a lot of time there, building the argument of his life. He had little else to do. Noodle shops, the market, and desultory chess with Mr. Loc from Ha Bac, a big wheel in air-conditioning.

And he had been to the war museum, twice. Tunnels, photographs of tunnels. You could fire the old weapons. It was depressing. He didn't believe in history, he didn't need to. He was twenty-six and brilliant, a lawyer already, and a Fellow. He specialized in harm. He was weighing offers. Boston, L.A. – Vietnam was the pause.

❋

She was a dental hygienist, she said she was. It didn't put him off. They weren't dating, but they met often – in parks, his car, her father's boat and, once, in a graveyard. Her English was excellent.

She spoke it rapidly, with force, like an adding machine. That took some getting used to, but her skin didn't. It was incredibly soft and exuded the fragrant dampness of bruised petals.

The first time he saw her he thought she limped, but it was just the way she walked. They were in the roof bar, under the stars. She was one of them, a deity, he said. She took off an earring and dropped it in his drink.

It went from there. They were many strangers. She brought the grease, he spun the wheel. She had a blonde wig. He wore surgeon's gloves. She was the actress with the hopeless past, he was the fisherman home from the sea. She was Jewish, he was a German, and drowning. They lit cigars and set money on fire.

The strange thing was, she always brought her brother. He smoked all the time and had a problem with his face, his smile. It was barely there, yet never far, much like himself. And he had someone else's hands, a much larger person's. He lugged them like packages. Otherwise, he seemed normal.

He drove the car. It was the time of Tet. Red banners, firecrackers. They were laughing in the back seat. Scooters whined by. Her feet clasped his neck. Don't move, she said, and called to the brother. He stepped on the gas. Move! she said.

Another night a storm staggered in, across the bay. They were in the father's boat, dancing to the radio. They had taken opium. The taste was spruce gum. She toppled to her knees, and the kimono slid. Everyone glowed. The brother tied the blindfold.

The further they went, the further there was to go. There were reasons to stop, but not strong ones. Until Dalat.

They made it up on the way, while he stroked her neck, the ridge-line of bone. She was the adulteress, sly and vicious. He was the husband destroyed by hope. They stopped at a mall; she stole the stockings, and he bought the flashlight.

They bypassed the city, its cowboys and paddleboats, and drove into the highlands. As they climbed the air cooled, but not much. The brother complained, in English; he was not himself. Hours between cigarettes, demanding the bill at dinner, and earlier, on a straight stretch, he had run over a bottle. They had to change the tire.

She knew the way. He didn't ask why. The valley came and went, and the same village. They could smell the pines. Darkness dropped.

Here, she said, and added something sharp to the brother. He turned onto a side road under an embrace of branches. The road changed to dirt and descended. The brother lit a cigarette, and they were there.

They parked. The brother stayed in the car. They went over the wall, into the graveyard. It was an ancient place, so lush it seemed at once to breathe and be still. She removed her shoes, kissed him, and fled. He waited. Then he hunted her.

She was lithe among the trees, the swales and hillocks, running, hiding. The flashlight was the game. Each time caught, she paid. Except the white stockings; they stayed on, and disappeared. He listened for her feet. It didn't take long.

He found her on a mound, splayed like a butterfly. He put down the light so it would shine upon them, and crept forward. The rain beat them. They felt nothing, heard nothing, only the glut of their breath. The mound had become mud. Then the light jerked away, and darkness crushed them. They flung apart.

The beam swung wildly, then tilted up. They saw the ghost of a face, its lip bleeding. A tire iron flashed, and she made a sound beyond sound. The brother stepped forward, and switched off the light.

He was lucky, and he knew it.

He left the next day.

※

She got married that summer. It was a large wedding, traditional. She was pregnant, and the man by her side, the silent phantom with the enormous hands, was not her brother after all.

A year later, in the dining room of a private club in New York, somewhere about the middle of a pointless joke (he was still junior man, so he had to laugh), he started to cough, and he kept on coughing until something small and fatal in his brain exploded.

It had been there since birth. He hadn't known about that either.

Saskatchewan

Tim Danes Jr., deputy police chief, recently named in the misadventures of the mayor's son, slapped his wife at the bail hearing, then hanged himself with a corset in a holding cell. It started there and spread, so that by the end of the week the ordinarily immured and turbid town of Lemming was under siege from within, and it wasn't even Christmas.

The former owner of John's Taxi, now Sam's Taxi, roped an engine block to his lap and drove through a bait shack straight into the river. The same day, the widow MacKenzie, having at last accepted Ed Fulton's proposal, rejoined her first husband, leaping from an overpass. Then the Connells, once socially prominent, took an overdose of their nephew's insulin in a double-mortgaged farmhouse full of cats gone feral. A drifter dropped a hundred dollars and a watch in a tithe box, and drank a quart of naphtha; Lois Finney, pregnant again, couldn't reach the trigger, so she grabbed a bared wire; Bob the Greek left a note no one could read and turned on the gas. Then Shawn Arnold, who had not in a decade missed a day, pepper-sprayed a Chihuahua, ignited a bag of mail, stripped naked, and took a slow walk at noon in the public pool, where he stabbed himself in the heart.

That was when he quit, Jules Gibson.

He decided in the shower, his third of the night. He threw on the blue suit he'd never worn, stuffed his things in a duffel, and taped a bad cheque for Mrs. Wu to the mirror. Then he went out the fire escape into the late empty dark and made his way to Munk's Funeral Home.

By dawn it was done: he had sloughed the makeshift of his life like a snake molt and slid off down the fillet blade of a prairie highway, shining at the wheel of a hot-wired hearse. It was an 80s model, a reconditioned V-8, and he was flying in rhythm, running changes on the gears. He hadn't slept much lately, but he felt great, as if he had punched a hole in a wall and squeezed through. How far he'd get, or where he was going exactly, Jules wasn't sure. The locks were still tumbling in his mind. But he had a full tank of gas, a fist of bennies in an urn in the dash, some suit-pocket ludes, and a six-pack sweating on the seat. Every ten minutes he pitched a can at a sign. He hit the first two.

Jules was counting roadkill when he saw her, this solid apparition hanging her thumb out. He slewed over, no idea why, and kicked open the door.

— East, he said. Make up your mind.

She gave a hard squint at the hearse, then leaned down and struck a stare in at him.

— How far? she asked. She had a sandpaper voice.

— Until I smell the salt. An older, wiser man was speaking for him now, some ancient sage who had eaten smoke and suffered visions. All Jules had to do was listen.

She shrugged and swung in. He thought at first she had a harelip, but it was just split, and she wasn't bad looking in a big-boned, Scandinavian sort of way. She carried a leather satchel that seemed heavy, and she stashed it between her feet. One arm was scraped, not too badly, but there was blood on her blouse, over her left breast, about the shape of Italy.

The plague was still growing.

They took off. Fields and feedlots, a turbine or two, and the flat open nothing. She wasn't a talker, and that was fine by Jules. She smelled of the stuff you rub on horses, and that was fine, too. He was used to strong odours and it swabbed a space in his head. He didn't ask about the blouse, then he did.

— You don't want to know, she said.

Miles died in silence. A strand of hair fell in her eyes. She didn't move it. A few transports blasted by. Then Jules saw a herd of cows that didn't seem to have heads.

— You see that?

— What?

He knew enough to say nothing. But the black beauty was going rodeo now with the beer. The road was vibrating like a plucked string. He shut one eye, and it helped, but not enough. He popped a lude and held on. He was thinking wrong thoughts not his own. They all led to a bad place. He yanked himself back, and started talking.

— What's the worst thing you've ever seen?

— Today, she said. She didn't look sideways.

— I hear you. Me, worse thing I ever saw was this woman. Last summer, we had that wicked heat wave, remember? Maybe you weren't living around here then, I don't know. Old woman, she lived alone. Melted into her couch. Maybe that's the worst, but it's got some competition. I'm a cleaner, when I'm not painting signs. I like painting signs, but it's small towns out here, there's only so many signs, you know what I mean? So I'm a cleaner, for this funeral home. Used to be. It's been a hell of a week.

Jules glanced over. She knew how to listen, like she wasn't even there.

He kept talking. Technical details: bleach pens, Virkon, kitty litter, the danger of carpet strips. Then he said the wrong thing, that he had his kit in the back and they could get to work on that stain, maybe. She was getting a free ride, after all. The woman didn't see it that way and started cursing in tongues. Jules tried to out-yell her. No dice, she dialed up higher.

She was digging in her satchel when the wise man spoke. Jules stood on the brakes and the woman's head slammed the dash like a cannon-ball. He dragged her out his side, she didn't resist much, and he sat her in the road. Jules went back to the hearse, tossed the satchel out the window, and drove away. He'd kept her kitchen knife. It was long, with a whippy heft. She was better off without it. He saw in the rear-view that she hadn't stirred yet. He guessed she would when she needed to.

Jules thought he had handled the situation pretty well, considering. But the great feeling was leaking, draining fast – out of his right ear, it felt like. He stobbed a finger in and thought of the Dutch boy, wondering if he'd drowned.

Then Jules heard a song he didn't like, direct from childhood, but the radio wasn't on. It made no difference. There were cigarette burns in the air, and char pieces broke off. He watched them drift, far up. Then it seemed they were hawks, and he tried to imagine how they looked at things, that exact precision. He couldn't.

The hearse left the highway, jumped a ditch, clipped a post of a casino billboard, and plowed through an electrified fence. Jules woke up in a pasture, dry-mouthed, and his neck hurt. The windshield was a shatter of nicks and spider-lines, prismed by the sun. He waited for advice, but the wise man was silent. Jules got out and sat on the hood. Horizon to horizon, nothing moved.

Jules took stock. It wasn't pretty. He was a hearse thief, sweating beads in a stupid blue suit, middle of nowhere. He'd have to change his name again. Maybe he'd say he was Russian, Dimitri something. He knew enough to get by, if there weren't any real Russians around. Or maybe he'd try the freak route, shave his head, eyebrows too, and pass as a mute. That sounded good. A life of silence, somewhere off the map.

He started walking.

The Tarn

It wasn't a long service, and before it was through
Dave thought he knew where Reid would be,
where he shouldn't be then, up at the tarn.
Bridget didn't think so. She was Dave's wife. It
was such a waste, she said, and the rest, well, it
wasn't worth the chase. He should let it go. She
told him this in the parking lot, in a low voice; it
was a small town. At least change your clothes,
she said. But he had already decided, and she was
used to that.

It had been five days. They had called a few
times, left messages, and finally driven over. The
porch light was on, but the truck was gone. The
second time they took the newspapers, it seemed
the thing to do. (They didn't leave a note, didn't
think of it till later. And a card would be more for
them than for him.)

Shad Corcoran had seen him when the liquor
store opened up, long enough to say hello and
start to tell him he was sorry. Reid waved and
kept moving. He seemed the same, Shad said. Just
apart in himself, and quiet.

Bridget drove Dave to the mountain. On the way they agreed again that the family was bearing up well, so well it jarred. Darla had been the youngest. Big-eyed, stylish, smart; different than the rest, and better. But blood is blood, and she was of theirs, so they had first claim and last. Yet it was strange to see them. Their placid gravity, the slow nods they gave as though the whole clan was one, and the ancient, undeniable grace of their faces. Still, the Sullivans, whatever else, were people of faith, informed that day by more than they were; and surely, if that didn't lessen pain, it simplified it, and excused a great deal.

She let him out by the side of the road. A couple hours, he said, more if it couldn't be helped, and then he would call her from the gas station, or else hitch a ride home. Dave watched her go and felt suddenly exposed and ridiculous in his suit, a mannequin plunked in the wilderness. He took off his tie and put it in his pocket, then jumped the ditch and started up.

It was an old fire trail, steep and root-wracked, thick with leaf litter. It would take a while. But the smell of the woods was a clean smell and it was peaceful to be back, climbing in the tall quiet, away from people. He wasn't in a hurry now, and he thought vaguely about a lot of things, small and large, but not what he would say to Reid. That would have to come to him.

Five or six years ago, just after he moved to the area, he had spent a lot of time on the mountain. Reid had a cabin there, not far from the tarn. They had hunted together, mostly ducks. Cold wet dawns, and a thermos of coffee and rum. Reid carved a few decoys and screwed on metal plates to keep them righted, though half of them sank. They got their bag limit, or they didn't. It was more about the company than the killing.

Dave didn't hunt now. Not from any dislike or rejection; it was just that those sorts of pleasures, like most worth the trouble, have their best days, and those days had moved on. Dave had taken over Kilkenny's plumbing business and married Bridget, so he wasn't as free. Reid got a regular job with the Parks Department, monitoring bears. The pull apart was slight and natural, a little wider over time, as could happen to the tightest joins.

When he came to the oak that bore a bole like an old man's face, Dave stepped off the path and, grabbing branches where he could, slid down the bank. The tarn glittered softly through the trees, and he emerged into the clear. It felt good to be right, as if it proved something.

— Mr. Mitchell, Reid called out. Come on over. He was sitting, knees drawn up, on the jut of a gravel spit, propped against a boulder. He wore a mackinaw, red and black plaid. He hadn't shaved. There was a quart bottle beside him, two-thirds gone.

Dave walked up past some beer cans smashed and strewn, the black remains of a bonfire.

—You look like a lawyer, said Reid. Whose side you on?

—Side that pays, Dave said. The good side.

—Have a seat anyway.

Dave folded his jacket, and sat on it.

—Been some time, wha'? Since you been here.

—Too long.

—Flying along. Want a drink? asked Reid.

—Straight's a bit much.

—Cutting back? Johnny likes company. Reid shook the bottle. I'm asking.

Dave shrugged and took a drink, and set the quart between them.

—Help yourself. I got more at the cabin.

—Staying there?

—Yeah. Roof fell in, you know.

—I remember.

—I put a tarp over. It's good enough.

—No rain anyway.

—Nice days. Hay weather. How's the business?

—More than I need. How's the bears?

—One less. I had to shoot it. Campground. I'd shot him before, with a dart that time. People won't pick up after themselves. Everybody's careless now. I'll have a cigarette if you got it.

Dave handed him one. Reid bit the filter off and spat it. He always did that when he was drinking. They smoked and looked at the water, the sky, the contrail of a jet. Then Reid tapped Dave's arm.

—Spy that vireo? In the snag there? He pointed to the cankered spire of a beech that thrust through the poplar and spruce, and above them. There was no bird.

—Don't think I do.

—She's there. All day. She's been watching me. I make her nervous.

He spoke that way sometimes, laying down planks, with space between. You could leap along, or wait. Dave waited. They had another drink each, and Reid another, and some minutes passed. They were settling yet, sizing who they were with each other.

It was deep afternoon now, the calm kind of late August day when the year turns back to the core of summer, and takes you with it. The sun had reached the treetops and the light streamed, throwing dapple down. A little breeze stirred the water. A dragonfly flicked by. The woods could do that, Dave thought, absorb and hold you, empty in a pause. He could smell the sweetgale.

—Tell me something, said Reid. You believe in the devil?

—Depends.

—What on?

—I don't know. The day.

—Today, then. Seen him around?

—Sure. Last week. Horny fellow. Getting gas at Richie's.

—Last week? Me too. Saw him in a taxi. He looked happy. Give my regards, you see him again. And tell him I'm coming for him. I'm gonna slit his throat.

Reid gave a laugh, short and harsh. He stubbed out his cigarette, and stood.

—I need a flat one, he said. Thin edge. He picked up a couple of rocks and side-armed one across the water, a dozen daps, a necklace. Then he fired the other high. Listen, he said.

The rock fell straight and hit straight, with a sound that was part punch and part tearing.

—Hear that? Hear that *thuck*? One slit devil. Gone to Meat Cove.

Reid stood still a moment, as if he were listening again. Then he snatched a rush stalk, and broke it off. He whipped it on his leg, the aimless way a boy might, wondering what to do with his body next. Or he was just drunker than he seemed; he should be, Dave thought, but he could drain a vat before it showed, then close down quick. Some long nights had ended so, back when they did that.

Reid threw the stalk in the water. He turned his palms up and looked at them. Then he turned and looked at Dave.

— How'd you know I'd be here?

— Wild guess.

Reid shed his coat and sat down. He reached for the bottle but didn't take it, and blew out a breath. And you're not a wild man, he said.

— Not lately.

— How's everything homeside?

— Better.

— Worked it out, huh?

— The way it is, that's all.

— Things change, you know.

— Some things.

— Yeah. I always liked Bridge.

— She's fond of you.

— Sure she is. Fond as hell.

— You're wrong.

— Doesn't matter. I wouldn't be either. Reid raised his left hand and touched a finger with his thumb. See the tan line? I got rid of it.

— Rid of what?

— I was sitting here today, looking at it. And I thought, I don't want to look at this ring anymore. What was it supposed to mean? We weren't getting married. I told her from the start.

So I got rid of it. Reid nodded toward the water. Two years. Devil's ring now. I never wanted it.

—I don't believe never.

—That's you. I never wanted it. What do you think of that?

—I don't get it. None of this. I'd like to, but I don't.

—Yeah, but what are you thinking right now?

There wasn't going to be a good time, so Dave said it.

—You should've been there, Reid.

—I *was* there. In spirit. Didn't you feel the cold breeze?

—Right. Forget it. It's your business.

—I appreciate you coming up here, Dave. I do.

—Any time.

—But that's not where I should have been. Down there. With the family, the sad Sullivans. Front row. Left side. By the stained-glass window. Picture of St. Jerome, helping the lion. I know that church pretty well. Before your time. My dad was a deacon, and I played my fiddle in the loft, when he died. Hard gig. And I dug the grave. I did. Broke the shovel, too. Now this time, though, this time I should've been where I wasn't. Understand? Then I wouldn't be here now. And neither would you.

—Make some sense, man.

—I'm making all there is.

—Not to me.

—The house! The fire! The goddamn Sullivans and their goddamned electrical fire! Just had to do it himself, didn't he? Suther the handyman. Cheap bastard. Couldn't wire a chicken coop, but he'd do his own place. What did he ever touch he didn't fuck up?

—You couldn't have known.

—And Darla stays over. She hated that house. A hundred things could have stopped her. I could've stopped her easy. She was lonesome. Don't ask me why. One night over, had to be that night. And the rest out drinking, lit like Christmas. *Now* I should sit with them? Look old Suther in the eye and shake his hand? No. The house is where I should have been. Dragged her out of there or died trying.

—Come on, Reid. Don't think that way.

—I don't think, I *know*. You want to hear where I was instead?

Dave shook his head. It was hard to look at Reid now.

—Well, I was nice and comfortable in the back seat of a taxi. With Red Clifford's girlfriend. You know her, legs up to here. And I was trying to figure out, does she have panties on or not? That's me. Where I was, what I am. Now you tell me that's all right. Try to tell me that.

Reid's face was still savage, but his voice had fallen. It wasn't a demand, it wasn't even a question.

—I can't, Dave said. I can't tell you anything.

It was true for each, and they knew it. Reid nodded. They had come to a limit that wasn't going to move, and a weariness with it. Dave waited, not long, then he lit the cigarette he'd been craving, and gave one to Reid. Reid tucked it behind his ear. Dave put the pack by the bottle.

The sun was low, the tarn golden now. Dave was hot and his legs were stiff. Reid squinted. He was staring, or shielding, or both together, although the light wasn't in them. He ran his hand heavy through his hair, back and forth, and down his neck. There was a different silence. Then a smile cut Reid's face.

—I'm all right, he said. Thanks for coming. But I owe you something. About my ring. I still got it. In my pocket here. Maybe I'll keep it, I guess I will. Don't know why I lied.

—I didn't hear any lies.

—That's good. I like that. You're a fine lawyer, Mr. Mitchell. You can go now.

—I could stay, too.

—Ah, I'm no company. And someone's waiting for you.

—She knows where I am.

—What I said.

—How about you?

—I'll stay a while. See the sun down. Go on, now. Couple of weeks is duck season. Maybe I'll give you a call.

Walking away, Dave wondered if he should have stayed, and gotten drunk with Reid. Maybe he should have searched out more of his own to give, but he had no feeling for what it might be. Or maybe he shouldn't have come looking at all, and Bridget was right, just not the way she meant it. It was a waste, all around, enough for every- one, wherever they should or shouldn't be. But it was gone beyond knowing, chasing shadows like that, so he let it go.

Magday

No one's out, then someone is. Down the ramp, through the dervish leaves, there is someone listing in the wind. A woman. She tugs her cap, and at the curb she stops to stare at her feet. Her sneakers, separate things, turn her in a circle twice, shuffle steps, arm across her chest. Mag, is it?

❊

Mag. She is old Mag today, because the wind weights her slow and the street is sad. She heads to the park, a mile off. Inside her coat, between her breasts under the sweaters and shirts, she carries bread. A whole loaf, from the Home. No one saw her take it. A week she waited, because the Omens said no until this morning.

Now it is clear. That's her luck.

The wind is rough, full of dust, butts, and paper cups. She frisks her coat. She does it fast, because her hands are hers. Her legs are Mag's, old today, and they drag like bricks. She starts the walk.

First, the lot with the chain across. It's where she finds her pebbles, three or eight (never nine), round ones with eggs inside. They are under the blue car jacked on blocks. Glass bits on the ground there diamond when there's sun. Hunting once, she sliced her hand. She didn't mind. The sky was wild shining that day. Now, it's blear. She hopes she is not too late, that her brood will not be gone.

Beyond the lot, the rainbow houses, all the colours. She tots the numbers, spits the nine. Last in line's a carcass on a slab. The porch is gone, the roof is air. She sniffs the char. Some boys lit it up for fun, late in the night last summer. Sirens shook the quiet. The street ran snakes and ladders, and the dark was flicked with bright. A woman burned – her hands, her hair. She rocked in a blanket. The cat got out, the fat yellow tom with the torn ear. She's seen it slinking, mewling in the ruins. Mag lets her feed it sometimes.

Next the wall, low and slate. Girls stroll it cold. Their legs are sticks and the men's faces steam. A graveyard lies behind. The headstones are split. To pass, she must add Mag's breaths and subtract the cracks: today it makes a five. She doesn't have to spit, only tap her teeth ten times with her tongue.

At the church, she halts in an alley by the bins where the wind is less. It's quiet there, except the vane above that's a dove, but skreaks. Inside at Christmas, hymns are clean and brittle like ice in bracelets on the trees. If she went, she'd wear her dress. The mauve one someone gave her. She keeps it at the Home, in the closet on the nail.

She'll be there soon, at the park, past the lights and through the gate. When she's in, Mag is out. She'll cast the bread upon the pond and call their secret names. They'll come in a squad then. She loves their greed.

She tugs her cap and goes.

A can bangs by, and in a gust a swipe of sand. On her right, an elm that's caught a kite. On her left, the store. Crates of apples prop open the door. The owner sits inside and smokes, thumbs a book of bare thighs. She knows because she went in and took a loaf once, put it under her coat and walked out. Mag must have told. He watches her go by, from his eyes that are slanted slits.

The mansion now. Seven pillars white as spines. How many rooms? God knows. Lions at the drive protect. To pass, she must touch their manes, then their jaws. A child stood there once, between the lions, crying. She rubbed his head to heal him, but he ran and hammered on the door.

The pub, the school, the billboard torn, the flapping hand, the barber shop that's boarded up.

Next, the tower where a thousand live. A cage of glass slides up the side. Birds reel about, in spirals and hooks. She stubs her toe on a rut and stumbles. The loaf falls out. She wipes it off and stuffs it back up.

The sidewalk curves, and then, there it is: the squat red box on midget legs. Inside is where she nests her pebble eggs. Three today. One for her, speckled and a whorl, and one for Mag that's black. The third, the pretty with a vein, is for her brood. She rolls them in her palm. She strokes them, and licks them, then tips the slot and drops them in. They clatter down, and ping. They should plop! The man with the key and the bag has been! The Omens didn't say.

The sidewalk dips. She trundles down and in. Under the overpass the wind is gone. The tunnel thrums. It smells like fish. She bites her tongue or Mag would hiss. Then she's out and the wind is back, swatting down the hill, up the flat in fists. It wraps around her like a wrestler. She batters through, toward the gate. There's only the cross-street in her way.

She must shut her eyes now, shut and step out. She does, straight into the street and roar. That's one. Then the second, stepping blind into the hole inside the wind; three steps and four, where the roar is still. Five steps, six, she tugs her cap, but the wind hits hardest there, and the cap is gone. At seven she forgets to clasp, and the bread slides out again.

She stops and drops. The pavement beats her knees. She gropes until the loaf finds her, rolling to her hand. She stands and steps, number eight. At nine, horns sound and tires screech. Mag laughs and the Omens scream.

※

By the park gate, a man is out. Young, well dressed, his hair is freshly trimmed. He looks like the lawyer he thought he would be. His cigarette won't light, so he turns and hunches, then hears the horn.

When he looks, it's over. In the middle of the road a car is stopped, then several. The wind blows glass and leaves along the pavement.

He steps on the cigarette, and re-enters the park. Through the gate, down the gravel path, he strides past the duck pond and the stiff swaying reeds, hurrying to tell his wife of only an hour that he saw a woman fly.

Mating

Martin and Diane, the Barrs, they were teachers. He was Math, she was Guidance, the same school. It was a good match. Everyone said so. She read books on Eastern religion, and ran several miles each day in the dark before work, in rain, snow, whatever. On the whole he respected that. He liked to lift weights and fool around with motorbikes. He kept half a dozen in rotation. Apart from the expense and the claim on space, she didn't mind. Neither drank to any extent, or desired children or cats. He stopped smoking in her presence. They shared a love of Indian food.

The ceremony was mid-February, a country church. Twenty attended – her people, and colleagues. His parents sent a wreath of begonias, a cheque, and a Bible verse. It was a long way and they were almost elderly. The recording equipment malfunctioned, but Alice from History was in fine voice. When it was over it was snowing so hard they could barely see.

The marriage lasted two years.

Two years less a day, thought Martin. It was not his thought, but the remark of a friend, Allen, who was single and caustic and had signed the registry. When the grading was done he might give him a call, go for wings and beer. Three inches, the disappointing senior class, remained on the dining table that was his desk now, surrounded by boxes. They were overdue, but the department head was relaxed about that, and the students inured. Besides, the May sun was shining, he had slept late and well, and grading was a simple task. Right or wrong, same every term. That was the beauty of math, and a pleasant way to pass a Sunday afternoon, his final in the house.

The door to the backyard was sliding glass, and when he stepped out to have a cigarette, he noticed a feather stuck in the screen and white daubs on the deck. He looked up. A mud jug, nearly complete, sat under the eave. So the swallows were back. Well. It was still his house. The broom would reach that far. He'd take care of it later, or tomorrow, when he mowed the grass.

He stubbed his cigarette in the ashtray, Allen's wedding gift. It was free-standing and huge, like a sculpture. He'd had to drag it from the shed.

He could hear the birds now. They were somewhere in the spruce, he thought. Did the male sing, or was it the female? Diane would know. His quick, sensible, fending wife – he still made that error – had a tender spot for birds, which was fitting in a way, because the last time they moved in, she moved out.

The separation, which he had waited for her to initiate, was clean. No wreckage in the closets. No one fell apart. They had given what they could, and accepting that was the price of truce. For a few months the house was neutral ground, then school started and she took a leave. Of absence, as they say. The relief was mutual.

She went abroad. A co-op farm in Umbria, a month in the Tibetan clouds, and now it was Greece, an island. There were more postcards at first, but the last said the most. She was sharing a house with two men. Tee was from Thailand, a wizard at sewing. He made his own jeans and Hugh sold them on the beach. They were wonderful people, better than the weather. Tee showed her ikebana, in which heaven and earth were one skinny tree, and man a leafless twig. She was up to twelve miles a day, but had hurt her shoulder rowing. She taught ESL under the dome of a whitewashed chapel to quiet, dark-eyed children. It was enough to live on, and she was thinking of staying. So would he, *as soon as possible*, sell the house please?

He would. He did. It was just a bungalow, nothing special. They hadn't put much into it but it sold in a week, above asking. The buyers brought their children for the second viewing, and their children's friends, and a couple of dogs and someone's parents. It was like watching a float go by in a parade, and he had never liked parades that much. It was theirs next Saturday, so on Friday he would have a touch of flu. (It was arranged. Tom owed him classes.) What he had not sold or given away by then would be in the van by noon.

His new place was an apartment. Ground floor, dark, on the small side. He would share the yard with the guy above, a dockhand who worked nights. The garage was his, and big enough for the bikes. They were there already, with his tools and weights. He had his eye on another Norton, a '68 Scrambler, practically mint. It might need a new seal around the kick-start shaft, but that was usual. Some new saddlebags, and he could make the Beartooth in July, do the poker run.

Travel was good. You could be anyone you liked, or someone you didn't; it wasn't supposed to last. He had been to Nashville, and to Florida a couple of times. Daytona Beach was a blast.

And Australia had been a passion once. He still had the books. Why not? It was possible. The money from the house would cover it. Next summer, maybe. Rent a bike and head south from Sydney, a slow month into wine country, then hit some beaches. Or cut inland, toss the map and see what came.

He would be forty-two then. It was a meaningless number, nothing to deny or plan for. Just more wear on the tires, his father would have said. Yet his father was a man who, by that age, had made and lost a million dollars, found God, shot the biggest buck in the province, twice, and stayed married for a quarter century. The first son, Wayne, became a missionary doctor in Kenya. Between sermons he ran a clinic for the blind, and along the way had sired the twin blonde angels of everyone's life. The other, himself, Marty the athlete, had painted the whole house, inside and out, when he was sixteen, and had never been a source of trouble.

He looked at his watch. Almost four, five their time, so he put in the call. His parents were fine, he was fine. It was not raining there either, and no, a photograph of the apartment wouldn't be too much to ask. After that he heated some soup and ate it from the pot, standing.

It should have worked. He wasn't selfish or inflexible. Neither was she. There had been no one else for either. They were the same age, the benefit plan was excellent, and what few quarrels surfaced were brief and of little worth. If she finished his sentences and got them wrong or too rarely laughed, and if at times his natural reticence shaded into silence and the trick of ease was put away, then that was not unusual, or even important, in the run of things.

It should have worked. It failed, so he had failed. It was a child's equation, he knew it to be so, and yet every so often he believed it. In part at least; he had that capacity. But most of the time he felt, obscurely but acutely, that the core of his life, its essential armature, had been mislaid, and that some day, when he wasn't looking, a kind of pause would open and he would be allowed to reclaim it. The sense this made was tenuous and variable, but not much more than anything else, and it got him through some nights.

The first months he had done some stupid things. Cocaine with the soccer coach on a field trip; and at three in the morning, after Jilley's closed, he racked up a bike, the Beemer. (He was lucky there, just some scrapes and bruises and no charges.) Then there was the improbable mistake with Alice, which had put a strain on them both, but mostly her. All that seemed long ago, and the marriage with it. Another life, said Allen, but he was wrong. It was a wild season, and it could happen again, for different reasons, or no reason at all.

He could use another cigarette, but he was cutting back. He made coffee instead and sat the cup on the finished pile. There would be some long faces. The mother of the Mullins boy would require an appointment. She would remind him that mathematics was one thing, but a child's sense of self, that was measureless; so he would have to tell her again that he could not agree more and, by the way, the child was nineteen. Round and round, a sad little dance, it could wear you out if you let it.

The noises of the house, how long a weekend was – the lightest things had been the heaviest. This past week, packing up, he felt it again. It was only a moment, while he was wrapping glassware. At least it wasn't grief, and not longing, either; he was through with that. What came back now and took its place was simpler and smaller and nameless. Even his private image, each time it returned, jarred further into doubt and dropped its features. Was it that way for her? Had it always been so? He had no idea.

The grading was finished. Seven failures, only one a surprise, but there was always one. She was smart, confident. Her father was a surgeon. She would probably cry.

He snapped an elastic around the stack, stuck it in his briefcase, and leaned back in his chair. The swallows had emerged, chasing another feather on the deck. They didn't seem good at it yet. The buffet of their efforts drove it on and away. Then one of them grabbed it and they disappeared, up into the nest they must be lining now. There would be a mess in the morning, and the mornings after for a while. It wasn't his problem. Let the new people decide. It was mating season, after all.

Bloodgrove

It was planned. Boxes and lines on a butcher-paper scroll. Which pallet had the smack, when the Mex watchman got paid off. Something like that. Supposed to be easy – snip a wire, in and out, half an hour tops.

The killing was extra, according to Ed.

He came over this morning to pick up some scrips. See, I do a little printing. Quality work, not enough to get noticed. He was all excited. Had it fresh, he said, before the cops let it out. Straight from Pris. Of course from Pris, but I wonder what her game is, where Ed fits in the jigsaw. However it cuts he'd better watch his back, playing with Pris.

She lives down there, in the Shambles. Hard in the heart of it. Booze cans and crack shacks, clip joints, all the sweets. She owns a strip club now, lock, stock and pole. The Paradise. Used to be a funeral home. Still got that solid plush feel. Class place, best lap talent here to the border. So they claim. I don't visit since my accident.

Steady Ed goes every night. Too bad, because he'll end there, under the docks. Some foggy dawn, with the gulls screaming. There'll be sand in his ears. I don't say anything. He'd just laugh, think I'm this crazy crip jagging on pills.

And maybe I am. Some days I believe it, with what I've seen. Bad dream pieces, twisted bits.

It started when I was racked up in hospital, eight years ago this fall. Tubes and traction and all the rest. Sucker odds on breathing much longer, and did I want to, even? Anyway, I was laying out one night, corked on morphine, watching the drip bag drain. Same blank night as a hundred others, except suddenly it wasn't.

Tough to explain. There came these lights, jacklights. Stiff in my eyes, jumping red. I could smell my brain. Hello goodbye, I thought, something's blown. I didn't bother with the buzzer. But whatever it was, some type of seizure, maybe, it cleared. And then I saw it, graved in my head stark as life. This flicking scene, ragged technicolour, lasting ten seconds, fifteen: a bald pudge guy, with a sleeve tattoo, was playing cards. Metal table, metal chair. Guy spread his hand and smiled, couldn't resist. A lop smirk he seemed to sip at, whichway teeth. Then an ice-pick voice said, This is for Reuben. Fatso looked up and thunk, thunk. Half a face left, spatter on the aces.

They're all like that. Lights, the dirty smell, then the scene. Bloodgroove stuff. A burned red-head in a ditch, the truck that threw her there. A stomping in a parking lot, gang on one, behind a mall. And an old man, he looked old, scrambling up an embankment with a child-size crutch for a prop. He made it and started down the track, the horn loud as hell.

A few more – a dozen? Twenty? I don't count. Did they all happen? Some did. Some others, not yet. Same difference for me. I'm used to it. Keeps me company.

Eight years is a long time.

See, I ran a garage, a triple bay bought and mostly paid, with living quarters attached. Across from the wrecking yard. Convenient. I stripped a lot of cars. Some legit work, too. Pretty good life. I didn't want more.

Then Pris blew in, like a drift of glitter. What can I say? We hit it off. Need on her part, she didn't have a dime. That didn't last, and neither did we. I was low rung and she was made for climbing. Nothing personal, never is with Pris, even when it is. But where that's flung I let lie, as a rule. Lynx eyes. Hard to think she's nearing forty now.

And mixed up with Ed. She's fast to dazzle, but I don't get that. He's a good kid, too. Not the sharpest knife, but reliable, for a booster. He hardly ever shorts me.

Funny, though, how paths cross, criss-cross and double back. Because I knew his dad. Frankie, Frankie damn Puryear. Kaszinskis were boss then, the twins, had their knuckles on half the state. They tapped Frankie for a comer. Petty strong-arm, then boom, he's Mr. Big. Silk tie, diamond stickpin. The whole flash deal. Mean slice of work. Kind of animal punk wasn't beating some-one, he didn't sleep right. Can't say I miss him.

Pete Chung took him out, a bouncer at the Paradise. Big dumb Pete with a mason's ham-mer. Common knowledge around the Shambles. Messy reason named Nola, Pete's wife. Hell on high heels, no question. Riddle was, still is for some, how did Pete – who couldn't find his ass with a map – find Frankie alone, when he always travelled in a pack? That is, who tipped him when and where? Same person Frankie thought he was meeting? Two a.m. or so, alone and re-laxed, under the Gramercy Bridge. Strange place for Mr. Big. I think I taste perfume. Or maybe Pete got lucky. Could be, and maybe I'll live to a hundred.

Pete didn't. Bang and done, rainy evening hit-and-run. September. Driver unknown. No description of the car, officially. I'd guess a black Buick LeSabre, whitewalls, new make.

The phone rang, two quicks and a long, and I let him in. Shakey, a born-to-lose pimp with a tic in his cheek and a leak in his pocket. He liked dog fights and owed deep all over. But he showed a grand. It looked real. I pumped for two. Not a quibble, he was one scared puppy.

Headlights and fender, new paint and plates. He smoked a reef while I worked, tic snapping overtime. It got on my nerves. Shake, I said, you don't need to stay. He scrammed. In fact, he vanished. Where to, I can't say. Safest bet's a lake bottom. Pris might know, they were pals.

At any rate, she wound up with the Paradise. On Frankie's dough. He was bankrolling it, laundry purposes. Pris was the front. Her name on the deed, tax reasons. That's another thing I don't tell Ed. Why rake coals? It's only the way it goes, in the Shambles. All the stories have holes, the true ones. Always.

Take this warehouse special got Ed so hot. Panic moment in the dark, or one guy got greedy and popped the other two? Had it planned going in, and if so, who with? Or decided on the fly? Or there wasn't any third guy, just the two cold ones. Cops will solve it, or they won't. None of my business. I'm out of it. I talked my way out.

I made a couple of tapes, like I'm taping this. When I was in hospital. Names, dates, iron facts, and some guesses. I connected the dots. It's enough. Sent a package to a lawyer, out of state, with specific instructions. Then I advertised. That's why I'm alive. My mistake was not doing it early, before the accident. Didn't think I had to. Then a truck dropped on me. Who did it, I don't care. A few bucks and a thirty-stone, there'd have been a lineup.

Anyway, how I look at it now is, it's already happened. I've lived my death. So I'm in no hurry. There's a raft of people cheering my health, one in particular. Almost makes it worthwhile, these eight years of hanging on. I'll let it drop when I feel like it. Because, right here, in this apartment I never leave, I've seen it happen. About like this:

I slide the glass. A warm salt breeze is blowing dust in from the balcony. I wheel my chair to the rail. Great view of the Shambles. I could pick out the Paradise if I wanted.

And there is, I swear, a blizzard of stars. Every last one shooting.

Downstairs

I

From the ground down there to where I live are
sixteen steps. I know them all. Number seven's
split, and the last is soft. Rotten. You have to be
careful. They can't say I'm not. I hold the wall. All
winter I do. The garbage hardens in the can, but
the cold takes the smell away. The tree has brittle
arms and leans, like me. Sounds are longer. The
birdhouse bangs. You can hear a dog for miles.

Red and yellow leaves hide the steps each fall.
I get the boy who clears the snow to rake them
up. No, it's Jill that gets him. She pays him. He
doesn't come sometimes. Then it's Jill, or the
wind will do it. I don't care. Let them stay. The
leaves, and me – just let us be.

In the spring it rains, and then you have to
watch your feet. I lean on the wall because my
hip is like glass.

Summer's best. My birthday's then, Orange
Day. There's a big parade, and where I live is full

of air. I smell the grass. The tree is straight. Sun-light stays. You needn't watch and hug the wall that shines. Or keep the count, up and down, six-teen steps until you're in or out.

Winter's worst, but I'm here and I'll stay. Four rooms are mine. That's enough. They can't make me go. I'm not a child. They want me gone because I'm old. Eighty-five. What's that? Not a hundred. I'm not daft. Daft is not knowing. When they come, I'll tell them. My head's not soft. It works. I manage. I know who I am. I am a married woman. I have three husbands. They are all downstairs. In the parlour.

No one's up but me. The light is like a plum. I wasn't tired, so I didn't sleep.

It's snowing. Look at it come down, like some-one ripped open a pillow. It was snowing when I wandered, too. I wanted a reason to be tired then, so I went for a walk. That's not wrong.

I'll sit here a while, then make my tea. I have a hundred cups. In every room there's some, in all the colours. Jill bought me one when she was just four, four or five. It's the blue one, china. She picked it out of all the others in the store. I dropped it once and it smashed. Everything might. You have to be careful. My husbands glued it. They had nice hands.

They won't get in. I won't let them. I'm not a child. I don't cry. They have it against me that I wandered and forgot. They have that, but I was tired. When I'm tired and should lie down, sometimes I don't want to. It's how I feel.

I liked it snowing, all the fluff. I wasn't cold. I had my coat. No I didn't, but I took my muff. Don't they think when I'm cold, I know? I do what they do then – I turn up the heat. They should know that. I wasn't lost. I didn't slip. It was late. I remember. The night was still and the snow was like talc. It melted in my eyes. Everything slept.

Then red lights came flashing behind me, and two men got out, and shamed me. They said it was wrong to be out and put me in the back. They drove us looking through the streets, but I forgot. I had to sit until I knew. I live at home, I told them. We drove. It was sticky where I sat. One of them laughed. How could I do that, forget where I live? In the car the night was darker. The window fogged. The houses slid by. None were mine. They went too fast.

They found Jill's number in my purse. Then I was here inside. No, not yet, not in. Sixteen steps. I fumbled at the door. My hands were numb things, nubs. They dropped the keys. Then Jill was there. She let me in.

There's the kettle, I'll make the tea. Where's the blue cup? Not in the sink.

The kitchen's clean. So what if I burned the crust? Anyone could. They have it against me because there is nothing inside them. Their mouths are holes and they're hollow behind. They wouldn't eat the pie. I baked it to show them I was me. Here, I said, I made this pie. Me. I made it for you. All they saw was I forgot the berries. They hate me, they do. I let them see I forgot the berries and now they hate me. They think I don't know.

I'm not daft. If I am, they'll grab me and take me down and leave me. I'll scream but my voice will be powder and blow away and no one will hear. I'll tell them I love them and they can't, but no one will hear. Then I'll be there in the dark. I'll be downstairs. That's what they want. I won't go.

II

I know how they went. I remember my husbands. They got up in the morning and sat down in the kitchen and they ate the breakfast. I made them all pies. No, I did not. I don't know what I made, but they ate it and they left and went downstairs. Then they were all electrocuted. I never saw them again because they didn't come back. I waited but they didn't. I was pregnant then. She cried all the time. I remember. I was young and Harold touched the wires and Jill cried night and day. She was big and I was young and it hurt to have her. No one was there when I screamed and she cried night and day.

I had to clean houses to feed us. There was never enough. On my knees I'd rub, wipe, and scrub. My knuckles bloomed and wouldn't fit my ring.

Then I was married again. He was good to me. I didn't care he was loud, or the mine came with him home on his skin, in his hair, the creases by his eyes. Everywhere black from the coal. Everett kissed me when I washed him. The tin tub.

It smelled of apples, what we did then. Apples and ferns. I didn't mind he was loud and threw the clock through the window. He rocked Jill in his arms, quiet and asleep, and I didn't have to scrub to feed us. Then he went and touched the wires.

No, it was Harold in the wires. I remember. The wires were alive so Harold wasn't. It was winter. Drifts to the eaves. He froze. That's right. He touched the wires and hung in his strap. He was blue on the pole and he hung there where they found him. They had to chip him down.

We were married in the flowers and I wore my mother's dress. She let it out to fit. I thought

they'd know, but no one did. Then we rented by
the station. Wind came right through the place.
And we had trouble with the roof, and put out
buckets. Underneath, it smelled. A skunk. My
husbands chased it out. What else?

Our bed was brass, slung with slats. The
wheels shrieked. He took them off. We were
young. He said my nipples were like baby's
thumbs and around them were two moons. Jill
was in my belly waiting. She wouldn't come till
spring. I wasn't sick, not ever. He put his hand
where she kicked. Outside was cold. The train
horns lowed, and the moon shone.

Who was it found him? Elmer? Elmer Green?
Odd I don't remember. Whoever it was, he ran.
Elmer ran from the pole, all the way to town
through the snow to his hips he ran and fetched
the others. They had to chip him down. I remember that and forget the rest.

I'm tired. Some things forgotten stay that way.
I'm glad they do. It's only what happens. It isn't
right or wrong.

III

Winter stays too long. Short days and the wind
shouts. You have to wait it out. Just look at the
icicles. They drip and lengthen down. Every year

there's more. Children snap them off and suck the prongs. I did. I skated, too. Fast around the pond in my red coat. Falling didn't matter then. The boys would snatch our hats, come up behind and skate away so we'd chase them. They took Myrtle's hat the most. She was pretty but we were friends. Bobby Snair took mine. To get it back I had to kiss him. No one thought the cold was cold. Myrtle Miller was a flirt, but Bobby held my hand and we went round. I put my hand between his legs, he put it there. It was strange, like eggs.

Myrtle had no mother, she was somewhere else. Her father was the butcher. Miller's Meats. One thumb was gone. They lived above and he'd pass bologna to us through the grate. He had a woman come. Alice? She had an awful stye.

Zion wasn't special, Myrtle said. She'd go to a city, soon as she could, and marry a rich man. She wouldn't have any kids because she didn't like her brothers. And any dress she wanted, she'd buy from the catalogue. And have a big house, and a maid. And drop things just to see her pick them up. Myrtle was a wanting girl. She had a mind of hope.

She went away to have the baby. I never knew where.

The scar from Bobby's knee curved to his hip. He got it from some wire, stepping over and it caught. I touched my fingers up the line and held him in my hand. He shook. I thought I loved him more than me. I remember. Myrtle told me it was clean, soap and salt.

She did it at fourteen. Someone from away, in Zion for the summer. We went swimming. The lake was rough. I could see him through his shorts. Bobby wasn't there. I crossed my arms across my breasts, and her friend made a fire. They went into the woods. When they were back Myrtle's dress was wet. We sat by the fire. He had a flask and gave us some to taste. Bobby wasn't there and he said I had nice hair.

What else? I went eight grades to school. We learned about the cheetah, and I drew a duck. The books were in the back, locked in a case. They lined us up for a photograph. The boys were lousy and the girls skipped rope.

The schoolhouse was cold till the stove got warm. A girl brought an egg in and you could see the chick. The Christmas tree had ribbons, popcorn strings. Someone threw up in the room and it steamed on the floor. We had slates and chalk, then it was a pencil. I added up what they said to, and wrote out the rules. If you had to go, you waited. The privy stank and the flies were fat. When they let us out the boys played peggy, and we played jink-a-link and jacks. I drew the duck and coloured it and I won a contest once. I made a speech, I don't know what about, but I won and got a cup. Silver, with my name on it. Mother used it for sugar.

All I need is here. My cookies and preserves. My tea. Three bags are best, but one will do if I let it steep. They'll last till spring. I wish it would come.

Winter's worst. The snow in the wind is full of sting. It hits the glass. Hits and hisses, like a cat that's mad. When I'm cold I turn up the heat, or I open the stove. It's gas and the smell is like lilac. So what if I do that? It isn't wrong.

The birdhouse bangs, so they sit on the wire. Starlings, are they? Ravens? No, they're crows. Just crows. Why don't they fry? I knew a Starling once, Everett's friend. That's not a good name for a man. They should have thought of that.   I wouldn't want one in a cage. Jill asked but I said no. They need the sky. Why don't the wires fry them? They should. They're thieves. Anything that shines, and they'll steal your eyes. Five and twenty black ones make a pie. Who would bake with birds? I never did. But I killed the one came down the chimney. With my shoe. Jill got scared and cried. I said it was sick and couldn't feel, but she knew. Children do. They know a lie.

IV

My husbands had tubes in their noses. The sheets were white. The light was hard. They whistled when they breathed. No one heard them go. I remember. The smell was garbage. They shrank. I watched them go. They couldn't suck the straws, they tried and just couldn't. There was nothing they could do. Every day was the same. The bubble at their lips and their breathing. It was like a kettle, in another room. The bubble wouldn't break. There was only waiting.

The nurses reached in through the railing and turned them in their cribs. I wore high heels. Click, click, down the hall. Stupid. Why did I do that? Heels are for a party.

Then it stopped. The waiting stopped. I prayed it would, but when it did I didn't want it to. It's awful what we know, then it's over. You go on. You think you can't, but you do.

They were preachers. No. William was, just William. He was last. That's right. We were never young. He courted me with words. A year of words. He knew some long ones. His Bible was leather, big as a breadbox. You didn't carry it one-handed. He kept a tract inside. About a man who went to hell for a look, to see if it was real. He dipped his toe in the fire and it burned and he couldn't get back. It was good, William said, to be reminded of that.

What else?

I sang in the choir, back row. I didn't want to. "Rugged Cross," "Cleft of the Rock," those. And we sat out evenings on the porch. I made lemonade and he read me the sermon. The sun went down and he said about the sins and wilderness, the bush that burned, Moses and the rest. It was hard at first, his way of things.

And he was shy about the bed. The light was always out. Not like Everett, sudden, wanting what was his. William kissed me like a kitten. After months. We never did some things I knew. Harold's hands were nice and it was sweet and fast. His eyes were green, gooseberries, and the apple in his throat bobbed. I watched it from below, up and down, and the vein stood out. I remember. We were new and my hair was thick. A currycomb, he said. Then he went.

I didn't cry. My eyes were stones and I was dry inside. I had to be. I scrubbed and wiped. For Mrs. Tully. That's right. I scrubbed and wiped, and I sat her baby. She had it late, she shouldn't have. Its head was huge. He couldn't live. My mother was a baby too, the last days. She drooled. Nothing was real. She wore a diaper and wanted chocolate. Then she asked about the boarders. It's suppertime, she said. I told her they ate already. She was younger then than me. William said a prayer.

Swillem, Jill called him. She was funny. Sweet William, we said. She waddled like a pigeon. We let her ride her trike inside. Jill rode over my foot. It hurt so much I slapped her. She ran away and hid and cried behind the house. All of me I hated then, running after what I'd done. I know who I am.

She choked one time. I wasn't careful. Where was that? She was six. It wasn't in Zion, we took the train. I pounded on her back. It came out on the floor, a peppermint. Pink. She was only four. I remember. We went to visit Everett's mother. We had tea in her room. Her sister brought it, on a silver tray. Everett's mother spilled. She was sick and in the bed. Mints were on the table. We fussed with the sheets and didn't watch and Jill popped it in.

But it wasn't Jill said Swillem. She was grown and gone. Why do I forget? I'm not a child. I'm older than my parents.

V

It was *me* said Swillem. I told it to his ear. He couldn't hear. The wires made him deaf. Yes. It was downstairs, in the parlour. They put him there. It was bright but dark. Red curtains. He wore the suit he preached in, the double-breast I ironed neat and sewed the button on. It was loose. He didn't look him. His eyes were pins. No, I couldn't see his eyes. They stole them. I know what they do. They're crows and want the shine. They steal and give you glass ones back. Little beads on pins that glitter, but they're fake. The preacher stood in William's place. He said the things they say. I didn't want to hear. The hymns were new. My hat kept falling. We sat and stood. My hat fell off. Someone put it back. His hands weren't right. That's the way they do it, behind the curtain. They take your hands and give you someone else's. Yours, they hide inside. You're hollow when they're through.

They use a hose. Jill told me, but I knew.

VI

When they come I'll show them my food. Pickle jars, cookies, and the beans. I don't waste. Mother taught me. She had a strictness. She'd get the cleaver, make it blur and whack me with the flat of it. The boarders didn't like it. They can leave, she said. She held a coldness over men. I remember. She never showed me how to cook. Learn yourself, she told me, then it'll be all you'll ever know. Or it was my father said it? No, of course it was Mother. She was the cook.

Father was kind. He made the crib for Jill. He couldn't read or write. You didn't need to then, just an X in the chit book. He worked the woods, and in the mill. Someone fell there once. You had to be careful. Everett lost an eye from a chip that flew. They put a glass one in, so one was green and the other blue. I didn't mind. Who was it fell? He wasn't careful. The saw stayed working. My father swore. Goddamn, he said. Him swearing rang in my head. They should've closed the mill.

My father's name was Robert. People called him Bob. We kept horses. Mares. Marnie and Stella. I fed them apples from the tree. Stella was pied and kicked the traces. Bluestone cured her thrush. I played with Myrtle in the barn, behind the bales. When I was sick my father wrapped me in the sleigh. The horses steamed and I smelled them in the wool. Flakes in my eyes. The runners sang. The doctor made me cough. He tapped my back. She's like a stove, he said. You have to wait it out. I remember. He had a bristle beard. They gave me candy after.

Now I keep them in the frame. Every day, I wipe them from the dust. I'm older than my parents. They wouldn't know me.

VII

We lived in the Diamond, on the wrong side of Zion. Everyone was poor, so no one was. The mine was up the road, past the company shacks. They cleared the woods and sank the shafts. Half the town went down. Everett did. He liked it. No one bossed you in the shafts. You dug your pay. A miner you could tell a ways off, by his walk. Forward sprung, hanging his hands like he had something to lift. Everett's legs were like iron. When the men got together they perched on their heels. You'd see them at ball games, the side hill. Hours that way, talking and smoking. They looked like birds. That's right. I don't forget.

And Everett left before the light. I'd be up to get the lunch. Buttered bread, a slab of cheese. I made the bread and churned the butter. Now *that* was work. Then I laid a fire on and scrubbed the clothes on the board. I did preserves and I sewed and I darned the socks. Knitted, too. Sweaters, mittens. I could hook and purl, not drop a stitch. I shovelled the snow and fed the chickens. Everett killed them. I hung the meat up on the house, in a pot on a hook, higher than the dogs could jump.

I did all that and I'll tell them I did. I won't say about the pies.

What's there now, in the Diamond? Not a mine, it's closed. When Everett quit, the dark was in his lungs. He brought it with him to the mill. Everett hacked a thunder and the handkerchief was black. They didn't stop the saw. My father swore. Firman stacked in the yard. Mr. Nash kept the tally, or Elmer Green. Or he was with the railroad then, waving the flags. That's in the fog. Firman got cancer. His lungs were paper. He had gentle eyes.

Everett didn't. He had a temper, his Irish half. Drink stoked him and I wouldn't let him in the house. He drank it in the shed. Starling came by, with his fiddle. He could jump a tune. Handsome, too. Wrong men are, just ask a woman. She'll lie, but it's true. Everett snored the night out on the couch. We had a fight and he grabbed the clock and threw it out the window. Time flies, I said. He looked at me, just looked.

Then Starling hit a moose and things got better between us. We had Saturdays to dance, at the hall by the lake. Sunday was for home. We read the funnies – Moon Mullins, the Hooples. And Everett carved the cribbage board and drilled the holes. On the back were our initials. V and E for victory, we laughed at that. With Eunice and Firman, who lived across. They came to our house, we went to theirs. I brought devilled eggs and Eunice baked a cake. Eunice was skinny. She didn't look a woman, Everett said. No one drank too much. Those were the best days. Then we moved.

When was that? The murder year? I should know. They might ask. It happened down from the stone bridge, by the veer-off. Near where the knacker was. Watson, his name was. He drove a spike in their heads. They were useless old. Such a stink, it sat in your nose. And the daughter was odd. She wore a sack to school. Shame breaks a child. Her mother was dead. Her father was a hog. Watson. He waited by the barn in a rocker. Haw, he said.

What was I thinking?

I was thinking about the murder. That's right. It happened near the stink. They weren't from here. He kept money in a mattress, they thought he did. All for that. Who locked doors? They used a hammer. Then they were hanged.

Was that when we moved? I'll say it was.

No. The murder was before, when the war was on. That's right. I was married to Harold. He smoked a pipe. Tamped it with his thumb and slapped it on his shoe. The smell was like hay. I'd make coffee, black as the devil's boot, and he'd get that tar down him and go. We were living where? That's in the fog.

What else? I baked a pie and forgot the berries. Harold touched the wires. Then Everett came. Yes. Because of his eye, he couldn't go. I was glad. You couldn't get bananas. Not sugar or stockings, nothing you wanted.

I remember my life. It's only what happened, but it's mine. They can't have it. When they come I'll show them. Look, I'll say, my hands are clean, the bed is made. I won't say about the pies. No. I'll show them my preserves. There's no mould there.

They'll want to trick me to forget. When was William, how long ago? They'll smile and ask and I won't know. I'll say about the fog. Yes. It was heavy when I wandered. But there wasn't fog, only snow. Powder. So slow it seemed still. I was lost. No I wasn't. What else?

I was a woman early. I had breasts at twelve and bled that year. There. Do they want to know that? They shouldn't ask. Leave me alone. The bathroom's clean. I don't smell. They can't say against me that I do. I'll show them and they'll see. Look at the pictures, I'll say, I wipe them every day. And all the cans in rows. Look. I bought them and I stacked them. Beans, peas, beets. I'm not daft.

There are sixteen steps. The last is rotten. I'm eighty-five.

What else?

What else?

Acknowledgements

The following stories were first published
in these magazines:
"Grebec" *Dalhousie Review*
"Easy Living," "The Tarn" and "Saskatchewan"
Exile: The Literary Quarterly
"Mating" *Windsor Review*
"Before You Were Born" *Front and Centre*
"Sandcastles" *Event*

The author would like to thank
the Canada Council for its support
during the revision of these stories.

Jesus Hardwell was born in a hotel,
and has lived in many places.
He now resides in Guelph, Ontario,
where he is at work on a second volume
of stories and a number of plays.